HERE COME THE BRIDES...
An exciting trilogy about triplet sisters
separated at birth—but reunited by love!

MILLIONAIRE TAKES A BRIDE by Pamela Toth
Special Edition #1353—On sale October 2000

When charming rogue Ryan Noble set his mind on
taking a bride, he did just that. Trouble was, he
claimed Sarah Daniels...the wrong triplet! To make
matters worse, his *un*intended bride's irresistible allure
was stealing *his* heart.

THE BRIDAL QUEST by Jennifer Mikels
Special Edition #1360—On sale November 2000

Runaway heiress Jessica Walker went into hiding as a
nanny for handsome Sam Dawson's darling daughters.
But could the sheriff's little matchmakers convince
Jessica that their daddy was the husband she'd always
longed for?

EXPECTANT BRIDE-TO-BE by Nikki Benjamin
Special Edition #1368—On sale December 2000

Pregnant and alone after an unexpected night of
passion with Jack Randall, her childhood sweetheart,
Abby Summers resigned
Jack had other ideas—h
wife, and he wouldn't ta

D1515744

Dear Reader,

As the beautiful fall foliage, sweet apple cider and crisp air beckon you outside, Silhouette Special Edition ushers you back *inside* to savor six exciting, brand-new romances!

Watch for *Bachelor's Baby Promise* by Barbara McMahon—October's tender THAT'S MY BABY! title—which features a tall, dark and handsome bachelor who takes on fatherhood—and the woman of his dreams! And romance unfolds in *Marrying a Delacourt* as bestselling author Sherryl Woods delivers another exciting installment in her wildly popular AND BABY MAKES THREE: THE DELACOURTS OF TEXAS miniseries. Sparks fly when a charming rogue claims the wrong bride in *Millionaire Takes a Bride* by Pamela Toth, the first book in HERE COME THE BRIDES—a captivating new trilogy about beautiful triplet sisters by three of your favorite authors. Look for the second installment next month!

One tiny baby draws two former lovers back together again in *A Bundle of Miracles* by Amy Frazier, who pays tribute to National Breast Cancer Awareness Month with this heartwrenching novel. Fierce passion flares in *Hidden in a Heartbeat* by Patricia McLinn, the third book in her A PLACE CALLED HOME miniseries. And not to be missed, talented new author Ann Roth unravels a soul-searing tale about a struggling single mom and a brooding stranger in *Stranger in a Small Town*.

I hope you enjoy all of our books this month as Special Edition continues to celebrate Silhouette's 20th anniversary!

All the best,

Karen Taylor Richman
Senior Editor

Please address questions and book requests to:
Silhouette Reader Service
U.S.: 3010 Walden Ave., P.O. Box 1325, Buffalo, NY 14269
Canadian: P.O. Box 609, Fort Erie, Ont. L2A 5X3

PAMELA TOTH
MILLIONAIRE TAKES A BRIDE

SPECIAL EDITION®

Published by Silhouette Books

America's Publisher of Contemporary Romance

Special thanks and acknowledgment are given to Pamela Toth
for her contribution to the Here Come the Brides series.

This book is dedicated with love to my mother,
Dorothea Coles, from whom I've inherited whatever talents I
may have. Recently she celebrated a milestone birthday,
but she would probably throttle me for revealing her age.
Mom, here's to many more.

And to my husband, Frank, who brings me rainbows.

 SILHOUETTE BOOKS

ISBN 0-373-24353-7

MILLIONAIRE TAKES A BRIDE

Visit Silhouette at www.eHarlequin.com

Printed in U.S.A.

PAMELA TOTH,

USA Today bestselling author was born in Wisconsin, but grew up in Seattle, where she attended the University of Washington and majored in art. Now living on the Puget Sound area's east side, she has two daughters, Erika and Melody, and two Siamese cats.

Recently she took a lead from one of her romances and married her high school sweetheart, Frank. They live in a townhouse within walking distance of a bookstore and an ice cream shop, two of life's necessities, with a fabulous view of Mount Rainier. When she's not writing, she enjoys traveling with her husband, reading, playing FreeCell on the computer, doing counted cross-stitch and researching new story ideas. She's been an active member of Romance Writers of America since 1982.

Her books have won several awards and they claim regular spots on the Waldenbooks bestselling romance list. She loves hearing from readers, and can be reached at P.O. Box 5845, Bellevue, WA 98006. For a personal reply, a stamped, self-addressed envelope is appreciated.

You are cordially invited to the wedding of

~~Jessica Walker~~ Sarah Daniels

&

Ryan Noble

Reception hosted by Stuart Walker,

at the Walker Mansion,

Willow Springs, Nevada

Chapter One

Sarah Daniels peered into the big mirror and patted her upswept auburn hair with an unsteady hand. Her pale-skinned reflection stared back solemnly, but at least her earlier anxiety had eased a little.

"Unless you want the veil on backward, keep your mitts away from your head," Kelly Richardson, her attendant, kidded as she positioned the pearl tiara that matched Sarah's earrings. "Everyone's waiting for you."

"It's lopsided," Sarah grumbled.

"It's fine," Kelly contradicted. "If you'd sit still for five seconds, I'd be done. Didn't you get any sleep last night?"

"Some." Sarah stifled a yawn. Although she usually avoided anything stronger than aspirin, this morning she had taken a tranquilizer to calm her nerves. It hadn't helped, so she'd taken another when she first arrived at the church.

Was she making a big mistake in marrying Dan Richardson today or were her concerns merely pre-wedding jitters like Kelly said? Dan was a sweet guy, he and Sarah had a lot in common, she got along well with his family and she loved him dearly—yes, she did—but was that enough for a successful marriage? Was her longing to be swept off her feet unrealistic and immature?

Sarah tried to sit up straight as Kelly arranged her veil. Sarah's parents had both died a few years before and the wedding was going to be a small one, but Dan's mother, Rose, had wanted Sarah in a traditional dress and veil so Dan could wear a tux.

"Are you okay?" Kelly asked as Sarah struggled to keep her eyes open. She had only picked at her breakfast and now she felt light-headed.

"I guess I've got cold feet," she replied around another yawn. "Oh, Kel, what if I'm making a big mistake?"

"Even though Dan's my brother, I still think he's a pretty great guy." Kelly stepped back to survey her handiwork. "You two make a cute couple. You'll have cute babies. Quit worrying."

"You're right. He's the best," Sarah agreed. "It's just…" Her voice trailed off and she struggled to stay focused. The room was getting awfully warm.

How could she tell Dan's own sister that he didn't

stir the passion she'd always assumed was dormant within her, just waiting for the right man to ignite it? Would all that change once he was really her husband, or was she cheating them both? It wasn't Prince Charming she longed for, but the beast whose broken heart could only be healed by true love. Perhaps she'd read too many fairy tales.

"Just what?" Kelly prompted. With a concerned frown she had stepped back to study Sarah in the mirror.

Sarah shook her head. "Nothing." If only her mother were still alive. Sarah had been able to ask her anything. She glanced down at her hands, clenched together in her lap. She, Kelly and Rose had all gotten their nails done yesterday. Doing things together was such fun.

"Dan adores you," Kelly said. "Our parents love you and you're like a sister to me." She leaned down and gave Sarah a hug, careful not to disturb her veil. "You're just nervous about the ceremony. In a little while it will all be over and you'll be on your way to Vegas for your honeymoon."

The mention of her honeymoon made Sarah feel faint. Dan was her best friend, she reminded herself. His family treated her like one of their own. The rest would follow. It was time to put aside a foolish girl's fantasies and act like a mature adult.

She returned Kelly's smile in the mirror, but her lips felt rubbery. "You're probably right." She fanned herself with her hand, which was ringless. She'd wanted an emerald, her birthstone, for an engagement ring, but Dan thought matching bands would be more practical. "I'm awfully warm. Could I have a glass of water?"

"Sure thing." Kelly glanced around the dressing room. "I'll run down to the kitchen. Stay put. I don't want you getting wrinkled."

The minute Kelly left the room, Sarah reached for her purse. Bending over made her woozy, but she pulled out the letter she'd written Dan two nights ago, trying to explain her misgivings and the reasons she'd changed her mind about marrying him—the letter she hadn't been able to deliver. Deliberately hurting someone, especially someone she cared about, had always been difficult for her. Jilting him now, in front of his family, wasn't an option. She was trapped.

With a sigh, she unfolded the letter and was struggling to read the words swimming before her eyes when the door to the dressing room flew open. She hadn't expected Kelly to return so quickly. Had Sarah wanted to get caught? Still holding the letter, she glanced up and blinked in surprise.

A man she'd never seen before stood in the doorway with an agitated expression on his attractive face. Wearing jeans and a plaid shirt, he was dressed too casually to be a wedding guest.

Sarah got to her feet, sudden dizziness making her head spin. That second tranquilizer had been a bad idea.

The church basement contained several meeting rooms and she assumed the man was lost. "May I help you?" she managed to ask, although her tongue felt too thick for her mouth and her voice sounded far away.

With a glance over his shoulder, he surprised her by stepping farther into the room. "I have to talk to you," he said in a low, urgent voice.

The edges of Sarah's vision grew dark and she struggled against another wave of dizziness. She didn't feel at all well. "Who are you?" Her head buzzed as she fumbled for the back of the chair to steady herself.

The man's frown deepened, as if her question displeased him. "You can't get married until you hear me out," he insisted.

Sarah opened her mouth to ask him to leave, but before she could form the words, she swayed and the letter she'd been holding slipped from her fingers. Spots danced before her eyes and she lost her grip on the chair. Her knees seemed to dissolve as the light in the room went dim.

Ryan Noble watched in astonishment as the woman he'd driven like Hades to prevent from marrying someone else slid into a boneless heap of satin and lace at his feet. Now what was he supposed to do? She probably felt guilty for running out on him the way she had, but he certainly hadn't expected her to faint at the sight of him.

Organ music swelled from upstairs and panic prickled at the back of his neck. At any moment someone would come looking for the bride. What would they think when they saw her on the floor with him standing over her? What might she accuse him of when she came around, just to get rid of him? If he was ejected from the church, he wouldn't have the chance to plead his case with her. The wedding would go on as planned and the opportunity of a lifetime would slip from his grasp.

Kneeling down, he sandwiched her hand between his and chafed it briskly. Except for the slight rise and fall of her chest, she didn't stir. When he gave her shoulders a shake, she merely groaned softly in protest. At least her pulse rate was steady.

Ryan was running out of time. In the instant it took to process his options, his decision was made. The back parking lot, where he'd left his Jeep, was deserted. Surely the fresh air would revive her. Once she was conscious, he would make her listen.

Ryan scooped her limp body into his arms. She moaned, but her eyelids remained closed. Heart pounding with the fear of discovery, he stepped into the deserted hallway and hurried toward the exit.

Moments later, Kelly rushed back to the dressing room. "I'm sorry," she said breathlessly as she pushed open the door. "It took me forever to find a paper cup."

To her surprise, the room was deserted. Had Sarah gotten sick? She hadn't looked good.

Quickly Kelly checked the adjoining rest room, but it, too, was empty. When she came back out, puzzling over where Sarah might have gone, she noticed a folded sheet of paper on the floor. Curious, she picked it up.

Kelly's eyes widened as she read the handwritten

letter. "Oh, poor Dan," she murmured. "Sarah's bolted."

As Ryan barreled down the road in his Cherokee, he kept glancing at the woman beside him, scarcely believing what he'd done. He'd only put her into his Jeep so they could talk without her getting chilled, but when she'd merely grumbled and turned away from him, sinking back into unconsciousness, desperation had taken over.

Now they were headed toward his mountain cabin and he figured he was in big trouble. Since he'd probably already broken several laws, he might as well go the distance and hope his passenger wouldn't press charges later. The caretaker kept Ryan's cabin stocked with provisions, so they wouldn't starve.

Ryan swallowed hard as he steered the Jeep around a series of curves. They'd left the town of Bellville behind and were climbing steadily. He'd thought she would wake up by now. What if there was something wrong with her? Acting so impulsively was out of character for him. If she didn't come around in the next couple of minutes, he'd have to chance pulling over and checking on her again.

Sarah's first conscious thought was that someone had glued her eyelids shut. Her mouth was as dry as cotton and her head ached dully. She was in a car; she and Dan must be on the way to Vegas and their honeymoon. Had she slept through the ceremony?

The ceremony! She pried open her eyes through

sheer willpower, the bright light nearly blinding her as she did so. A groan slipped through her parched lips and her eyes scrunched back shut.

"Jessica, are you awake?"

The deep voice didn't sound familiar. And yet—

Abruptly she recalled the dark-haired man who'd come into the room, the one who'd insisted on speaking with her. She realized that his sudden appearance was the *last* thing she remembered.

Cautiously Sarah peeked at her surroundings. She was traveling in a vehicle she didn't recognize and she was still wearing her wedding dress, but one of her shoes was missing. A lump of fear rose in her throat. Had she been kidnapped?

A hand touched her shoulder and she cringed. "Hey, Jessica," the same male voice said, "are you okay?"

She debated playing possum, but saw no advantage in postponing the inevitable, so she turned her aching head slowly and looked at him. Even though he was driving very fast on a road she didn't recognize, he kept glancing at her with a worried frown. Perhaps she was worth more alive than dead. The thought made her stomach turn over.

"Who's Jessica?" she croaked.

"Very funny." His reply confused her, making her headache worsen. Had he drugged her? No, she remembered the tranquilizers. She'd drugged herself.

They rocketed around a bend in the two-lane road and she looked out the window, but all she saw was trees. "Where are you taking me?" she asked, and then she immediately started coughing.

The man reached down and handed her a water bottle. "Here. Drink this."

She glared at it suspiciously and then another bout of coughing overtook her. Eyes streaming, she grabbed the bottle and drank.

Although her head still hurt, full consciousness was returning rapidly and with it a jumble of questions. At least he hadn't tied her up. She debated jumping out of the vehicle and trying to escape, but they were traveling at high speed and the ground fell away from the road on her side. They hadn't passed a single other car and she hadn't noticed any buildings. Even if she survived the fall, where would she go?

Before she could decide, she heard the sharp click of the automatic door locks. Her captor must have seen her white-knuckled grip on the handle and guessed at her intentions. "Don't be stupid," he exclaimed. "I'm not going to hurt you."

"Then what *do* you want?" she demanded hoarsely. "Where are we going?" She took another long swig of water. When the road curved again, she could see mountains ahead. And snow. There were patches of it among the trees around them. "And could we please slow down."

"Why did you run away from me?" he asked, easing up slightly on the accelerator, but ignoring her questions. "Why wouldn't you give us a chance?"

When he glanced at her again, his gray eyes were intense. The set of his mouth was grim. Despite his forbidding expression, he was very attractive, with jet-black hair growing back from a widow's peak and cheekbones to die for. Sarah was quite sure she'd never seen him before in her life. His was a face she would have remembered.

Too bad he wasn't making a lick of sense. Oh, dear Lord, he must be delusional. Was he some kind of stalker? She swallowed, heart pounding. Or worse?

"Good grief." His lip curled with disgust. "Don't look at me like I'm a damn serial killer. All I want is to marry you!"

Oh, hell, he'd done it now, Ryan realized. He hadn't meant to blurt out his intentions quite so baldly, but she was staring at him as though he'd waved a knife under her nose. Maybe they hadn't been formally introduced, but she sure as hell knew who he was. Deidre had assured him that she would discuss the situation with her daughter.

"You what?" she whispered, her expression even more shocked than before.

"Jessica," he began in a more reasonable tone as he reached over to pat her arm reassuringly. To his annoyance, she shrank away.

"Don't touch me, and quit calling me that! My name is Sarah Daniels." Her voice had risen with each word until she was shouting.

"No, it's not!" he shouted back, frustrated. "It's Jessica Walker and we both know it. Just like we both know that I'm Ryan Noble, so quit pretending I'm some damn stranger you've never laid eyes on before."

When she didn't respond, he sneaked another glance at her face. His stomach did an abrupt nose-dive. Tears swam in her gorgeous blue eyes and spilled down her creamy cheeks. One caught in the corner of her full mouth, drawing his attention to her trembling lower lip.

A woman's tears were his Achilles' heel. "I'm sorry if I wrecked your wedding," he blurted, wishing she'd turn off the waterworks, "but you know it was a huge mistake. Marrying some guy you just met to annoy your grandfather is a lousy reason to tie the knot." Unlike Ryan's reason to marry her, which was a damned sensible one, but he refrained from pointing that out.

"What the hell are you prattling on about?" she snapped. "You might be right about my marrying Dan being a mistake, but it's certainly none of your business, and I don't even have a grandfather that I know of. I'm adopted."

This time when Ryan glanced at her, she'd stopped crying, her blue eyes were shooting sparks and there were angry red patches on her pale cheeks.

He ignored her last comment. She was trying to confuse him. "Of course you know who your grand-father is. He's the reason I'm here."

"And that's why you want to marry this Jessica you keep mentioning?" she demanded with a sniff. Her tiara was listing to one side and crying had left mascara tracks on her cheeks, but there was no doubt in Ryan's mind who she was. Lucky that the private investigator he'd hired to find her had spotted her photo in the local town newspaper before she'd hitched herself to someone else.

"I want to marry *you*, as you well know." He slowed to take a turnoff from the main road. "Do you always refer to yourself in the third person?"

"You've kidnapped the wrong woman," she said in a much more conciliatory tone. "Tell you what, you just turn around and take me back to Bellville. I won't press charges."

"First we talk," he said stubbornly. He hadn't gone this far—both literally and figuratively—to give up now. Besides, it wasn't as though he was a total reject. Women actually pursued him on occasion. He was already successful, with an even brighter future than he had ever imagined nearly within his grasp. Once Jessica got to know him and realized fully just how much was riding on their merger, he was confident she'd see reason. He had to believe that! Anything else was unacceptable.

With a toss of her head that nearly unseated her tiara, she sat back and folded her arms. "No," she said, her chin jutting stubbornly as she stared straight ahead. "I won't listen to anything you have to say. I'll put my fingers in my ears. You've made a big mistake and I insist you turn this vehicle around right now."

"You aren't Jessica?" he asked, deciding to play along with her just to see what she'd say.

She jerked her head around to look at him. "That's right, I'm not. I've never even heard of Jessica Walker, or of you," she added pointedly.

"So what's your name again?" he asked.

She heaved a sigh of relief that drew his glance to her lace-covered breasts. "I'm Sarah Daniels. I grew up in Bellville. Ask anyone who lives there. I work in the local bank. My best friend is Kelly Richardson, my fiancé's sister."

She was a quick thinker, he'd have to grant her that, and smart. But he was quicker, and smarter. "Prove it."

"What?"

"You heard me. If your name is really Sarah, prove it."

She glanced around the interior of the Jeep. "Where's my purse?"

Ryan shrugged. "How should I know? You must have left it back at the church."

"*I* left it!" she shrieked, making him wince. "You're the one who kidnapped me when I was unconscious! Couldn't you have grabbed my bag on your way out?"

He wrestled with his impatience. "Please stop using that word. I haven't kidnapped you. All I wanted was a chance to plead my case and I could hardly do that when you were passed out on the floor, now could I? I had no intention of bringing you with me. It just happened. Of course you can't prove you aren't Jessica because we both know you are." He glanced at her long dress. "When we get to the cabin, I'll loan you some clothes so you can change out of that getup."

"Peachy." She sounded petulant. "Do you carry a selection of women's sizes, or just mine?"

"No, just *mine*." He could be sarcastic, too, when he wanted. Privately he thought she looked like an angel in the wedding gown, but he wasn't about to give her a compliment when she insisted on being so uncooperative. Then he remembered something she'd said earlier. "What did you mean, your wedding was a mistake?" He hadn't expected her to admit it quite so readily.

To his amazement, she actually blushed as she glanced down at her tightly clasped hands. At least she wasn't wearing his rival's ring. Ryan would buy her a rock, if that was what she wanted. "I shouldn't have said that. It slipped out."

"Because you knew marrying that guy was a dumb idea," he said, satisfied.

She rolled her eyes, and then her shoulders sagged. "Whatever." The spirit had drained out of her voice. "How much farther to your hideout?"

They'd been traveling on a gravel road that had turned to a narrow snow-covered track a while back and they were climbing steadily. "Not far," he replied. Hideout, indeed! Despite its relative isolation, the cabin had cost him a pretty penny. It was his private escape from the pressures of business, but he'd never brought anyone with him before now.

"By the way," she asked, "if kidnapping me just happened, like you say, why did we come all the way up here to talk?"

Ryan slowed to turn into his private driveway.

"Dressed the way you are, I figured stopping at the local coffee shop might be awkward for you."

She stared in obvious disbelief. "Oh, right." Her voice dripped sarcasm. "The next thing you'll be telling me is you have no choice but to marry this Jessica person in order to save your inheritance."

Ryan pulled up in front of the cabin and stopped. He draped his arms over the steering wheel and stared at his passenger. Wisps of fiery hair had worked themselves free to frame her face and dark smudges circled her blue eyes. She was pale with exhaustion, fear or a combination of both, but her chin was angled defiantly and her lips were compressed as she glared back at him, as feisty as a cornered kitten.

"No," he said in contradiction to her sarcastic comment. "As you damn well know, the reason for our marriage is to preserve *your* inheritance, not mine."

Sarah could only gape at him in astonishment. She'd been adopted. Could he know something about her past that she didn't? She sat up straighter. Maybe she was the missing heir to a fortune and he was trying to take advantage of her situation. She'd been abandoned as a baby and no one had been able to give her any information about her background.

Sarah narrowed her eyes, trying to figure out a way to worm the information from him, and then she saw the obvious hole in her theory. He didn't even know her real name.

Disappointment deflated her like the prick of a pin.

She was back to square one, wondering if he was a harmless nut or a real threat.

"Don't you have anything to say?" he demanded. "Even though Deidre explained the situation, you must have some questions."

"Who's Deidre?" Sarah asked.

Ryan slapped his hand against the steering wheel, making her jump in reaction. "This is ridiculous. If you're going back to that pathetic act, we might as well get inside before we both freeze to death."

His words made her realize how chilly the interior of the Jeep had become without the motor running. Her bare foot, in particular, was getting really cold. The ground outside was covered with snow and she had no idea where they were or how far they'd driven before she woke up.

While she contemplated her situation, Ryan released the door locks and climbed out of the Jeep. She watched warily as he came around to open her door.

He wasn't exactly dressed for the mountains in his lightweight shirt and jeans. Maybe he'd been telling the truth about not planning to bring her up here; otherwise wouldn't he have worn a jacket and boots? Unless his warmer clothes were already inside.

He held out his arms. "Come on. I'll carry you." His expression was benign. Was he having some kind of erratic mood swing or did he actually believe, for whatever reason, that she was this other woman he kept talking about?

There was no way of telling how deep the snow

was or what the ground was like beneath it, so Sarah reluctantly leaned forward and put her arms around his neck. The movement brought their faces very close together. For a moment, Ryan studied her from beneath a fringe of thick, dark lashes. His eyes, she noticed, weren't just plain gray. The irises were an intriguing blend of silver and charcoal, each rimmed with gold like a wedding band.

Abruptly Sarah remembered Dan and the church full of people she'd left behind with no explanation. She stiffened as Ryan was about to pick her up. Under the circumstances, she was more than a little crazy to find him attractive!

"Now what's wrong?" He scooped her up as easily as if she weighed next to nothing, which Sarah *knew* was far from true.

"You've ruined what was supposed to be the happiest day of my life!" she cried as he carried her up the steps of an utterly charming log cabin nestled in the trees.

Shifting his hold on her, he entered numbers into a keypad by the door and then plucked a key from its hiding place. "Rubbish," he exclaimed as he unlocked the door and pushed it open. "You've already admitted that I saved you from making a big mistake, so don't try to lay a guilt trip on me now because I'm not buying it." He set her on her feet inside the cabin and headed back outside as she stepped out of her remaining shoe. "I've got to get my briefcase."

As he walked away, Sarah spied the key still sticking out of the lock. Without stopping to consider the consequences, she kicked off her remaining shoe and grabbed the key as Ryan glanced back over his shoulder.

"Hey!" he exclaimed, turning. "What are you doing?"

With a burst of triumph, Sarah stuck out her tongue, slammed the solid door on his startled expression and turned the bolt. Heart pounding, she looked around wildly, expecting him to start pummeling the door with his fists.

Instead she heard nothing as her gaze darted around the room in front of her. Figuring he was probably trying to decide which window to break, she barely noticed her surroundings except to search for a phone with which to call for help. By the time she figured out there wasn't one, she'd wasted precious minutes instead of grabbing something with which to defend herself. No sooner had the idea of finding a weapon occurred to her than the front door swung open.

There stood Ryan, wearing an expression that was an annoying combination of irritation and male superiority. He carried an expensive-looking briefcase in one hand and with the other he held up a key that was a twin to the one she'd taken.

"I always keep a spare," he said, advancing on her with intentions she could only guess at.

Sarah backed away from him warily. Trying to lock him out had been a stupid idea. It had probably made him mad. "W-what are you going to do now?" she asked, her voice hardly more than a whisper.

"The first thing is to get you out of those clothes,"

he drawled as his gaze traveled over her trembling form.

Her heart nearly stopped at his words, and then he pointed toward the short hallway. "You can use the bedroom while I get a fire started. There are sweats and T-shirts in the bottom drawer of the dresser, heavy socks in the nightstand. Sorry I don't have any boots to fit you."

He must have noticed the expression on her face, because his eyes narrowed and his cheeks turned a dusky shade of red. "I'm not even going to ask what was going through your mind just now," he growled with a fierce frown before he spun away. "If you're so damned determined to keep thinking the worst of me, I guess I can't stop you."

This time, when Ryan stalked out, it was his turn to slam the heavy front door behind him, leaving Sarah to wonder how, under the circumstances, she could actually feel guilty for hurting the feelings of the man who'd spoiled her wedding day.

Chapter Two

The bedroom Ryan had indicated was larger than Sarah expected to find in a cabin, even one as grand as this. The walls were made of logs that had been stripped of their bark and treated with something to give them a satiny finish. The ceiling had open beams. On the hardwood floor was a rug patterned in red, black and white. A matching quilt covered the bed that was too imposing for her to ignore. Did Ryan expect to share it with her?

Sarah gulped and searched for an escape route. Diamond-paned windows were cut into two walls. As she stared through them, her spirits plunged. Even if the small panes hadn't been divided by a grid of sturdy-looking black metal, she wasn't dumb enough

to think she could find her way through the snowy
woods surrounding the cabin, especially missing a
shoe. Had Dan found it on the church steps, like the
prince from Cinderella?

With a last wistful glance at the window that might
as well have been barred, she removed her tiara and
veil. After she'd pulled out the pins holding back her
hair, she fluffed out the stiff strands with her fingers
and hid the pins in a clay pot on the black dresser.
Maybe they'd somehow come in handy.

Opening the drawers Ryan had mentioned, she
found a pair of faded gray sweats with a drawstring
waist, a large blue T-shirt and thick socks to keep her
feet warm. A quick search revealed nothing in the
dresser but male clothing.

How much time did she have before he came to
check on her? Not wanting to get caught half dressed,
she decided to change clothes before she looked any
farther. Stripping off her ruined stockings and the lacy
white garter belt, she looked around for a place to
stash them. Finally she rolled them in a ball and hid
them under the bed. It was only when she reached
around to unzip her dress that she remembered how
Kelly had fastened it up for her in the church dressing
room. The heavy satin bodice was too snug for Sarah
to reach the hook at the back of the neck, no matter
how she contorted her arms and shoulders. After several more frustrating moments that made her joints
ache, she gave up.

For some reason, the uncooperative zipper annihi-
lated the last bits of her bravado. She slumped onto

the edge of the bed, chin wobbling, eyes filling with tears she didn't bother to blink away.

With the door shut and the woodstove cold, the bedroom was still chilly so she rubbed the goose bumps on her bare forearms and tried to think what to do. Her headache had returned, her stomach was empty and she had no idea how long her captor intended keeping her prisoner.

Dan must be worried sick about her. Had his family called the police? What had Kelly thought when she came back to fetch Sarah, only to find her gone?

Perhaps, even now, a SWAT team was gathering outside, prepared to storm the cabin. Hope rose in Sarah as she crossed to the window, still hugging herself to keep from shivering as she searched for stealthy figures among the trees. She couldn't tell if anyone was hiding out there, but if they were they'd see her.

If she got out of this unharmed, she would do things differently, she vowed. She would talk to Dan about her concerns instead of writing them in a letter she didn't have the nerve to give him.

The letter! What had she done with it?

Sarah pressed her fingertips to her temples. She'd been reading it when Ryan appeared in the dressing room doorway. She tried to remember putting it back in her purse, but she knew deep down that she hadn't. She must have dropped it when she fainted. Anyone who read it would assume she'd abandoned Dan at the altar and left of her own free will, a coward who couldn't face him with the truth.

She swallowed hard as realization hit. No one was searching for her. There was no SWAT team preparing to storm the cabin. After they'd read what she wrote, Dan and his family probably hoped they'd never set eyes on Sarah again.

She was on her own. Hysterical laughter bubbled up in her throat like acid when she realized she was actually relieved that she didn't have to marry Dan after all.

But at what price? And how was she supposed to prove to her captor that she wasn't who he believed her to be?

She struggled with exhaustion and defeat, eyelids drooping. A shiver danced up her spine, so she pulled an afghan from the foot of the bed and wrapped it around herself. The touch of it against her skin was as soft as a kitten's fur, as comforting as a childhood doll. Rubbing the yarn against her cheek, she swallowed a sob and debated her options.

The first decision she must make was whether to admit to Ryan that she couldn't get out of the dress without assistance. Maybe she'd just pretend she didn't want to remove it.

While she considered her best course of action, she swung her cold feet off the floor and tucked them under the afghan. It had been a long day. She needed food to keep up her strength. She needed rest so she could think clearly. With a sigh, she lay back on the mound of feather pillows as her stomach rumbled. She'd just close her eyes for a moment, and then she'd confront him.

* * *

By the time Ryan had built a fire, checked out the generator and heated a pan of soup on the propane stove, he realized that Jessica had been in the bedroom for quite some time. He'd already reset the security system so she couldn't have gotten away without making a lot of noise, but the bedroom was as still as a tomb when he pressed his ear to the door.

Perhaps she was sulking, although he'd hoped they could discuss the situation without any childish behavior on her part. It might have been a different story if she didn't know who he was, but Deidre had assured him that wasn't the case.

For a moment he considered the possibility that the woman in the bedroom *wasn't* the one he'd agreed to marry. Could he have made a mistake and grabbed her exact double? What were the odds of that happening?

No, she was either Jessica Walker or her identical twin, and Ryan knew she had no siblings. Even if he hadn't recognized her at the church, Stuart himself had identified her from the newspaper photo. As Ryan knocked softly, there was no doubt in his mind who was waiting on the other side of the bedroom door.

When there was no response, he turned the knob slowly and peered inside. As soon as his anxious gaze settled on the bed, he opened the door wider and eased his way quietly into the room.

Looking like a princess from a fairy tale, Jessica was snuggled under the blanket with her fiery hair brushing her cheek. She was sound asleep. Feeling like a voyeur, Ryan stood with his hands stuffed into his pockets and studied her curiously. Until today he'd never seen his intended this close, and earlier he'd been too busy driving to really look at her.

In repose, her face resembled a delicate porcelain mask, the creamy skin flawless, the features—each attractive enough in itself—coming together to form a whole that made his breath catch. She looked so peaceful that for a moment he was tempted to lean down and kiss her. Not wanting to frighten her if she should awaken, he pulled the blanket up instead. As he did, he noticed that she was still wearing her dress. Its V neckline gave him a glimpse of her cleavage. Despite her stubborn streak, being married to her would be no hardship, he realized with a start right before he forced himself to shift his gaze and ignore the primal awareness jolting through him.

The dress was tight; she had to be uncomfortable. Hadn't she found the clothes he'd mentioned, or was she just being stubborn again? From what he'd learned about her so far, he'd guess the latter. As long as that streak of obstinacy didn't interfere with his plans to marry her and cement his relationship with her grandfather, she could be as contrary as a cat on a leash.

Ryan didn't expect a love match, nor did he want one. From his observations, bringing emotions into an equation only clouded the real issues. He'd seen first-hand how forming a sentimental attachment could mess up a person's life for good. That was one stake-lined pit he planned to avoid. What Ryan did expect from Jessica for as long as they were together was loyalty and the same fidelity he would grant her.

She stirred on the bed and he froze, but then she merely burrowed deeper beneath the afghan with a tiny whimper. He didn't imagine she'd appreciate being spied on while she slept, so as soon as her breathing deepened again, he tiptoed from the room and eased the door shut behind him.

Patience didn't come easily and he was eager to start his campaign, but he wanted her alert when he talked to her, not cranky and uncooperative. Despite the urgency nipping at his heels like an unruly puppy, he forced himself to go back to the kitchen and turn down the burner under the soup. Then he took the opportunity to call Stuart on his cell phone with a progress report.

When Sarah opened her eyes, the room was dark and it took her a moment to get her bearings. She sat up slowly, the afghan sliding off her shoulders as memory returned. The air was still chilly and the woods beyond the windows had turned into an impenetrable black wall.

She pulled the socks she'd found earlier onto her icy feet as she gazed at the change of clothes with longing. Wrapping the afghan around her like a cloak, she padded to the door and listened. When she didn't hear anything, she tried the handle. At least Ryan hadn't locked her in. Perhaps he would feed her, and then it was time for a showdown.

Raking her free hand through her hair to untangle

it, she marched into the hall. A lantern glowed from a side table and she glanced at her watch, surprised to see it was only late afternoon. The sun set early in the mountains.

She didn't hear anything and, for a moment, terror rose in her throat. Had he left her here alone? The idea propelled her into the main room where a fire burned low on the hearth below a sweeping rack of antlers sans, thank goodness, a glassy-eyed mounted head. Sarah crept closer and loosened her grip on the afghan as the blessed warmth soaked into her.

A soft snuffle spun her around in alarm. Ryan was sprawled on a big leather couch, hands folded on his flat stomach, fast asleep. Her first impulse was to shake him hard and demand that he take her back to town, but then she reconsidered. Here was a chance to explore and perhaps to escape.

After a few moments, she realized that, even with the aid of the flashlight she'd discovered on a side table, she wasn't going to find anything that would help her if she was foolish enough to try leaving in the dark. The jackets, boots and other warm gear must all be secured in the one closet that was locked.

If Ryan had a cell phone, he probably kept it in the briefcase next to him, along with the keys to his Jeep that she hadn't been able to find. The combination lock on the elegant case appeared too sturdy to break without tools, even if she could have gotten her hands on it without waking him.

She watched him for a moment, chewing her lip. Did he own the cabin or was it rented? Although the furnishings she'd seen were appropriately rustic, even Sarah could tell they weren't inexpensive. The trappings of wealth made her even more curious about her host and the woman he'd mistaken her for.

In the modern kitchen a light burned and a pan of soup sat on the stove. The sight and smell of it made her stomach growl, reminding her that she hadn't eaten for hours, but the soup was cold. Biting her lip, she stared at the unfamiliar knobs. Reluctant to risk lighting a burner and blowing them both up, she tossed the afghan over a chair and looked in the refrigerator instead. The interior light went on and the inside felt cold. The contents appeared fresh.

For how long had Ryan plotted this little caper? Was calling her Jessica just a ruse to make her lower her guard? He'd insisted coming here had been spontaneous, but now she wondered.

Sniffing the orange juice cautiously, she poured herself a glass and tore open a package of cookies from the cupboard. Mouth watering, she took a long swallow of juice and bit into a chocolate chip cookie. Nothing had ever tasted so good.

"I see you've finally come around."

With a squawk of fright, Sarah dropped the glass, which shattered on the stone floor and splashed juice on her skirt. Fury blotted out her fear as she rounded on him.

"What the hell do you think you're doing, sneaking around like a ghost?" she cried.

His eyes were heavy-lidded and his hair was attractively messy. Under the circumstances, he should have looked menacing, but somehow he didn't.

"Sorry. I didn't mean to scare you." He rubbed a hand along his darkened jawline. "Don't move until I clean up the glass. I don't want you cutting yourself."

His concern diverted her until she realized a lame captive would no doubt be a nuisance. Deliberately she hitched up her skirt and stepped over the mess on the floor, turning to see his reaction to her disobedience as she finished the cookie.

With a frown of displeasure he grabbed a broom and a dustpan. "Suit yourself," he muttered.

Stifling the ingrained offer of assistance that leaped automatically to her tongue, Sarah dusted the crumbs from her hands as she studied him. His shoulders were wide without being bulky and the long muscles in his arms flexed like well-oiled machinery as he wielded the broom. "What do you do for a living when you aren't kidnapping people?" she asked when he straightened.

His gaze clashed with hers, but he didn't answer until he'd emptied the glass into the trash and wet a towel.

"I wish you wouldn't use that word," he grumbled as he mopped up the juice.

"What would you have me call it?" she snapped. "A blind date?"

He tossed the towel in the sink and lit a flame under the pan on the stove. "You know damn well your grandfather and I are business partners, so quit playing games. I'd planned to feed you as soon as we got here, but you fell asleep.'' He glanced pointedly at the open package of cookies on the counter. ''You must be hungry.''

Why lie? ''I'm famished.'' Her first need was for food, her second for an explanation that made sense, not the maddening bits of information he'd given her so far. ''It's been a busy day,'' she couldn't resist adding.

''For me, too,'' he replied in a dry tone she didn't know how to take. She supposed she should be terrified and wary of his Jekyll-and-Hyde mood changes, but right now she was just too hungry to care.

''Can I help?'' she asked, her hunger growing as he began pulling sandwich fixings from the fridge. Too bad she hadn't thought to grab a knife from the drawer before she'd been distracted by the siren call of chocolate chips.

''You could butter the bread and pour more juice,'' he suggested. ''Unless you'd rather a beer or some wine.''

Not sure if all the tranquilizers were completely gone from her system, she declined. She needed a clear head to outwit him. ''Juice is fine.''

Without asking, she poured a glass for him, too. If he preferred something stronger, that was too darn bad. This was hardly a sociable meal. Defiantly she thumped both glasses down on the table, aware of his quick glance in her direction and wondering why, under the circumstances, she couldn't seem to resist doing her best to provoke him.

"Didn't you find any clothes that fit?" he asked after a moment, glancing at her wrinkled dress.

"I need help with the zipper." Her chances of escape would be better if she wasn't hampered by the long skirt.

"I hadn't thought of that. Let me see it."

She shook her head. "After we eat."

When she'd donned the dress this morning, she'd expected to spend her wedding night in Vegas with her new husband. Instead here she was in a remote mountain cabin sharing a can of soup with a handsome stranger. And she'd thought her life was dull!

"Then you might as well sit down. Everything's ready."

Sarah didn't need a second invitation. Once he'd set a steaming bowl of soup and a sandwich in front of her, it was all she could do not to fall on the food like a dog.

"So tell me how you found me," she suggested after she'd taken the edge off her hunger. Maybe she could figure out why he'd grabbed her by mistake and use that to make him see the light.

Ryan swallowed the bite of ham sandwich he'd been chewing and drank some of his juice as his gray eyes studied her over the rim of his glass. With his looks, he reminded her of the bad boy from a daytime soap. "First tell me why you ran away from me."

"How many times do I have to say that wasn't me?" she groaned. "I'm not your Jennifer and I've never laid eyes on you before today."

"Jessica," he said mildly, "if you think deliberately getting your own name wrong is going to fool me, you're mistaken. As soon as you admit who you are, we can work this out.''

Sarah stared down at her soup as tears of frustration filled her eyes. Her appetite had fled. ''This is crazy. Are you planning to marry a complete stranger? Why don't you know your own fiancée?''

''If you'd stuck around, we would have gotten to know each other, wouldn't we?'' he asked in a reasonable tone that set her teeth on edge.

Irritation growing, she let her gaze wander over his face. Given his appearance, it was hard to believe that any woman would run out on him, until he opened his mouth and started talking nonsense. If he was crazy, he hid it well.

Sarah tried a different tactic. Leaning her chin on her elbows, she studied him thoughtfully.

''If I *was* who you think, I certainly wouldn't have left you,'' she said flirtatiously. She even batted her eyes for effect to see how he'd react.

Instantly Ryan reared back in his chair, his expression wary. ''What are you doing?''

Sarah shrugged and smiled. In real life she was rather shy, but she'd learned in high school drama class that as long as she was playing a part she could be who she wanted without feeling awkward. ''You must look in the mirror occasionally. Why would any woman walk out on you?''

''You did,'' he said stubbornly.

''Did I?'' she shot back. ''Are you sure it was me?''

For a moment he looked confused, and then his expression hardened. Had she provoked him too much? Before she could think of anything soothing to say, he scraped back his chair. "I've got something to show you," he said and then he stalked out of the kitchen.

In a moment he came back with a newspaper clipping and handed it to her. "Explain that," he said, sitting back down.

Sarah studied the engagement photo of herself and Dan. It was a flattering shot. Puzzled, she laid down the notice and looked up at Ryan. "What's to explain? It's a picture of my fiancé and me."

Expression triumphant, Ryan leaned forward and tapped the clipping with one finger. "Your grandfather identified you."

He sat back and folded his arms across his chest. The sight of his wholly masculine forearms, deeply tanned and lightly dusted with hair, nearly distracted Sarah until his smug grin jerked her back to the matter at hand.

"I told you I don't *have* a grandfather," she said with exaggerated patience. "If my parents were still alive, you could ask them."

"You don't have a grandfather and your parents are both dead? How convenient," he drawled.

Hurt and anger at his insensitivity filled Sarah. "Having your parents die when you're still in college isn't *convenient*," she contradicted with a quaver of emotion. "It's awful. I miss them every day."

The pain in her voice was so convincing that Ryan

nearly offered his condolences before he remembered that she was making it up as she went along. Jessica's father had died before she was born. Her mother waited for her return back at the mansion.

Tired of Jessica's lies, he slapped the tabletop with the flat of his hand. The dishes jumped and so did she.

"Why do you persist with this stupid story?" he demanded. "The sooner you admit the truth, the sooner we can go back to Willow Springs where we both belong."

When Ryan had called Stuart earlier, the old man hadn't been comfortable with the setup at the cabin. Despite Stuart's wealth and sophistication, he was understandably old-fashioned when it came to his granddaughter. Reluctantly he'd given Ryan three days to win her over, but that was the extent of the old man's patience.

"It's not a stupid story," she cried. "I belong in Bellville, where I grew up. Dan's family and the friends I left at that church must be worried sick. They probably think I've been abducted by aliens." She leaned forward, eyes narrowed. "The police are probably closing in on you right now!"

Ryan ignored the comment. He was reasonably sure no one had seen him make off with her and they certainly hadn't been followed or he would have been pulled over long before they got here.

"I'm sorry if they're worried," he snapped back, ignoring a jab of guilt for the poor slob who'd been stood up. It wasn't Ryan's fault the other man had been duped by her innocent act.

"Look, I'm not proud of grabbing you the way I did," he admitted. "It was probably a stupid impulse, but I had to stop you from getting married. I didn't expect you to drop at my feet, but when you passed out before I could talk to you, I panicked." He spread his hands. "And here we are."

"Okay, I understand," she replied. "Let's just go back to Bellville and we'll forget this whole thing happened. I swear I won't press charges."

Ryan was shaking his head before she'd even finished. "It's too late for that. What's done is done."

When she paled and sank back into her chair, he realized she had misunderstood. "Oh, no, no." He extended his hand, but she shrank away. "Don't look like that. All I meant was that I can't take you back before we work this out. I'm committed."

"You should be committed," she muttered as she lowered her gaze.

Ryan ignored her comment. "Your wedding guests have known you for what, a few weeks? They'll probably assume you had second thoughts." What kind of an identity had she created for herself and how had she persuaded her clueless groom to propose so quickly? She was certainly a fast worker, but a woman with her looks could send a guy's common sense to the moon.

Bright pink spots appeared on her pale cheeks. "My friends have known me all my life," she contradicted. "Except for going away to college, I've lived in Bellville since I was five and the Daniels adopted me.''

Was there no end to what she'd say to confuse him? This was getting them nowhere.

Ryan pulled out his wallet. Extracting a small picture that Deidre had given him, he slid it across the table. ''If you grew up in Bellville, what were you doing at the high school reunion in Willow Springs three years ago?'' he asked smugly.

He'd hoped she might slip up, but he hadn't counted on the extent of her acting ability. When she stared at the picture, he would have sworn the blood drained from her face as though she'd never seen it before. When she finally looked up, her blue eyes had darkened with emotion and her lower lip trembled. A nice touch, he thought cynically.

''Where did you get this?'' Her voice was hoarse. ''Whose picture is it?''

With a snort of disgust, Ryan got to his feet and began pacing. Maybe this whole thing had been a bad idea, not just the part about bringing her here so they could get to know each other better, but his agreeing to marry her in the first place. Despite the sizzle of physical attraction, he was beginning to question his ability to deal with her obstinacy on a regular basis.

He'd done well on his own; it wasn't as though he *needed* Stuart Walker or his money but, dammit, the old man had taught Ryan so much. Seeing Jessica settled was important to him. This was Ryan's one chance to repay Stuart's many kindnesses and Ryan hated the idea of letting him down.

"Is this Jessica Walker?" The subdued voice jarred Ryan's thoughts back to the present.

"You know who it is."

Still in shock, Sarah set down the photo with a hand that trembled. The picture looked so much like her. There had to be a logical explanation, but what? A cosmic joke? A coincidence? People said everyone had a double somewhere. All she had to do was to convince Ryan that *she* was Jessica's double.

Sarah studied him wordlessly. The light emphasized the planes of his face and the strength of his jawline. The fringe of his lashes shadowed his silver eyes, turning them smoky and mysterious. In any other circumstances, she would have wanted to know him better.

For a moment, she actually envied Jessica for Ryan's determination to win her. Dan was very sweet, but had he ever shown this much ardor? He'd never even proposed. When he and Sarah dated for a while, everyone, even the two of them, just assumed they'd get married. After being alone, feeling like part of a family again had been wonderful for Sarah.

Growing up, she'd been a solitary child with a lively imagination and her nose in a book. Was she in danger now of confusing her attractive captor with some fairy-tale hero she'd sighed over before she'd eventually decided it was time to grow up and be sensible with a steady man like Dan?

After a moment, Ryan shifted uncomfortably. "What are you staring at?"

An unbidden thought squirreled its way through

Sarah's mind. What if she stopped trying to convince him she wasn't Jessica and went along with him instead? Now *there* was a fantasy a girl could sink her teeth into! And once he was convinced, he'd have to take her away from here.

She must be losing her grip on reality even to consider such a crazy plan. She knew nothing about him and had no idea what he expected to happen while they were here together.

What if he wanted some form of tangible proof that she'd changed her mind about marrying him? How far was she willing to go to regain her freedom?

Not that far, she decided, not while there were other options. She'd never done anything spontaneous and irresponsible in her whole life, and now wasn't the time to start. Soon enough she'd be going back to Bellville to face all the people who thought she'd run out on poor Dan. Eventually the dust would settle and her life would return to normal—same job, same friends, same routine.

Meanwhile she had a situation to deal with. She folded her hands in her lap and gripped them together hard.

"Why don't you tell me what is it exactly you hope to accomplish by keeping me here?" she asked Ryan.

He leaned forward, his gaze locked on hers. "Like I said before, I want you to come to your senses, make your grandfather happy and agree to marry me."

Despite herself, Sarah was curious. He hadn't said anything about making *him* happy. Didn't that figure into his equation? "Why would an attractive, apparently successful man like you get involved in such a crazy scheme?''

Irritation crossed his face. ''It's not crazy. Your grandfather and I are partners in several complex business deals. He's not a young man and his holdings are extensive. He's thinking about retiring. Before that happens he wants to see you settled with someone who won't run his business into the ground.''

''That's archaic!'' Sarah burst out. ''It sounds more like a merger than a marriage.''

''Why can't it be both?'' Ryan replied.

Sarah was nearly speechless. ''What about love?'' she sputtered. ''That's why people usually get married these days, or had you forgotten?''

He made a dismissive gesture. ''And look at the divorce rate. If you ask me, romantic delusions are a weak foundation for marriage. Love is highly overrated.''

Sarah gaped at him. ''If I wanted practical, I'd marry Dan,'' she blurted.

As she clapped a hand over her mouth, mortified by her outburst, Ryan studied her thoughtfully. ''That doesn't sound like the love match you've been touting.''

''I'm not going to discuss Dan with you,'' Sarah huffed. ''How long do you plan to keep me here, anyway?''

''As long as it takes to persuade you.''

Her heart sank at his reply. ''Okay, fine, I'll marry you,'' she said flippantly. ''Now can we go back?''

Ryan's gaze bored into hers. "I don't believe you."

She hadn't expected that he would. "Then you've got a real problem," she pointed out.

"What do you mean?"

"How are you going to stop me from promising to marry you and then changing my mind the minute we set foot back in civilization?" she asked. "Even if you found someone to perform the ceremony against my will, it wouldn't be legally binding."

For a moment his face was blank with surprise. Clearly this little glitch hadn't occurred to him. He raked one hand through his hair, leaving it in untidy furrows. For some reason, it made him look vulnerable and uncertain. Under different circumstances, she might have actually felt sorry for him.

"Ready to give up yet?" she taunted instead. As soon as the words were out, she realized she should have put the query another way.

His jaw tightened, his expression mulish. "There's got to be a way we can work this out. Until I figure out what it is, we stay put."

Sarah slumped in her chair, disappointed. "Now what?"

He picked up the uneaten half of his sandwich. "I suggest that we finish our meal and start getting to know each other. Winter comes early in the mountains."

"It's April," Sarah exclaimed. "Next winter is months away."

"My point exactly." His tone was grim. "So tell me, what's your favorite color?"

Chapter Three

"My favorite color?" Jessica echoed, clearly puzzled.

Although Ryan finished his sandwich as calmly as though he were on a first date with a willing companion, his insides were churning. The silence following her question spun out between them; the only sound besides his chewing was a sudden pop from the wood in the fireplace. He'd have to add a log before it burned too low.

Jessica was right. Not only did he have no way of knowing whether she was lying if she did agree to marry him, but the deadline her grandfather had imposed dangled over his head like the Sword of Damocles. What the hell had Ryan been thinking when he'd hatched this crazy plan?

"Teal blue," she muttered, breaking the silence that had become brittle.

His expression must have mirrored his bafflement because she gave a feminine shrug and her gaze slid away from his. "What shade is that exactly?" he asked, grabbing at her response as though it were an olive branch.

The way her nose scrunched up as she considered his question was rather charming. "It's kind of dark, not a pastel, certainly, and it's actually more green than blue, I guess."

"Then why don't they call it teal green?"

Was it his imagination, or did some of the tension around her eyes actually fade? "Beats me."

"Ahh, I think I know what color you mean. It would look great with your hair." He spoke without thinking. The deep rich tone would turn the auburn curls to pure flame and her eyes to jewels. The poetic thought made him squirm, but at least he hadn't spoken it aloud.

"Thank you," she said with obvious reluctance. "What about you?"

"Me what?" he asked.

She rolled her eyes almost comically. "Haven't you been out much? This is how it works. You ask a question, I answer. Then I ask and you answer. See? It's called *conversation.*" She emphasized each syllable separately, so they came out sounding like four separate words. "Very simple, like lobbing a tennis ball. We find out we have nothing in common and then you take me home." She smiled brightly and batted her lashes.

Ryan's cheeks heated with embarrassment. She must think he was as dumb as a stump.

"I like red," he said, annoyed. "And black."

"So this really *is* your cabin?" she asked.

"Yeah, why?"

"It explains the color scheme in the bedroom," she replied as she spooned up some soup. "Did you do the decorating yourself?"

The soup had cooled off again, but he'd be damned if he'd reheat it for a third time. "My contribution was to describe what I wanted," he replied. "Someone else did the rest."

She looked disappointed as she nibbled on her sandwich. "Did you buy the cabin or have it built?"

He had no one to blame but himself for all the questions. He was the one who'd suggested they get to know each other. "I guess you could say I bought it from a guy who owed me money. I thought it would make a great getaway."

"Not to mention a place to stash all the women you abduct."

Ryan scraped back his chair and grabbed his dishes. "You make it sound like I do this all the time. I've never brought anyone up here until now, especially not a woman." He couldn't resist adding, "Either voluntarily or otherwise."

Her eyes widened. "Really?" She actually looked pleased. No wonder he was still single at thirty-five, he thought wryly as he put the dishes in the sink. Who could follow the workings of a woman's mind? Still, he wasn't about to toss away any advantage he could get.

"That's right," he said. "As a rule, I come here alone." His comment was met with silence. When he turned around, she was watching him with those big blue eyes as though she was trying hard to figure him out.

"What is it?" he asked gruffly. Such close scrutiny made him nervous. What did she see when she looked at him so intently? Women seemed to like his looks, but all he saw staring back from the mirror was an average guy with a bony face.

"It's so sad that you don't believe in love," she murmured, catching him by surprise.

"Oh, I believe in it," he nearly snarled. "I know love exists because I saw what it did to my mother after my old man walked out and left her to raise me and my sisters alone. He broke her heart and she never got over him." He jabbed a finger into his own chest. "*I* got to be the man of the family, but it didn't make much difference. She missed the old man. What I said was that *emotion* isn't something I'd want to base a marriage on. It's too damned unreliable."

She looked stunned and he suddenly realized how much he'd revealed with his outburst. He never talked about his father leaving, *never*.

"I'm sorry," she said quietly. "That must have been painful for you. Do you miss him?"

"No," he denied sharply. "My mother was the one who carried the torch, not me."

The way Jessica was looking at Ryan made him want to add that her own grandfather had been more of an influence in his life than his old man ever had, but he swallowed the comment. As far as he was concerned, dragging up old news wasn't the reason they were here. The fact that they'd both lost parents didn't make him feel all warm and fuzzy. If she thought he was willing to compare scars, she had a disappointment coming.

"Is your mother still alive?" she persisted.

"She died five years ago." Even then Ryan had reached a point where he could easily afford to make her life comfortable, but her health had been ruined by long hours of hard work. She had not lived long enough to see the enormity of his success.

"I'm sorry." Jessica bowed her head, genuine regret in her voice as her fingers formed small pleats in her skirt. "But you're lucky to have sisters, at least. Being an only child can be lonely."

"I'm sure that's true." She'd grown up cocooned by wealth and security. He would have traded an empty belly and a chronic lack of privacy for loneliness in a minute, but he'd already said more than he'd intended.

"Do you see your sisters often?" she persisted.

Ryan shrugged. "One is married, with two kids, and the other lives in Paris. They have their lives and I have mine." Before she could comment on that, he changed the subject. It was time to shift the spotlight away from him.

"You must enjoy your volunteer work, although I

didn't get the impression that your mother entirely approves,'' he said to divert her.

Deidre had made it plain to him that she didn't understand Jessica's unwillingness to lead the privileged life of the idle rich that Deidre herself so enjoyed. Instead Jessica spent her time working at a home for disadvantaged children. Although Deidre had been quick to reassure Ryan that ''Jessica's little hobby'' didn't need to be a problem once they were married, he respected her dedication and he intended telling her so.

Before he could, her chin went up defiantly. ''And what work is that?'' she asked in a snippy tone. She tossed her head and laid the back of her hand against her temple in a theatrical gesture. ''I seem to have forgotten.''

Back to square one, he thought grimly.

Getting to know each other was a waste of time as long as Ryan refused to believe who she was, Sarah decided, pushing her chair away from the table when he didn't immediately reply. There had to be some way to convince him, but what?

''Would you like to change your clothes?'' he asked as she hesitated, torn between a grand exit and helping to clean up the kitchen.

She searched his face for any telltale signs of uncontrollable lust at the idea of lowering her zipper, but his expression was merely inquisitive. Given the choice of comfort or stubborn pride, Sarah opted for the former. The fitted bodice and snug elbow-length sleeves of her wedding gown hadn't been designed for prolonged wear.

"Please," she said, "if you'd just undo the catch at the back of my neck and start the zipper for me, I can manage the rest." Without waiting for his reply, she turned around and bowed her head, lifting her hair out of the way.

The brush of his fingertips against the skin of her nape sent a shiver down her spine that she felt all the way to the soles of her feet. As she tried not to tremble, his indrawn breath signaled that she wasn't alone in her reaction.

For a moment he did nothing, his fingers still. Sarah remained frozen, half intrigued and half fearful.

"What's the problem?" she finally squeaked.

"Nothing. The hook's pretty small," he said gruffly as he fumbled at her nape.

He must have leaned closer, because she could feel his breath against her sensitized skin. Just when she thought she must either move away or arch up like a cat hoping to be stroked, he grunted, indicating success, and she felt the two sides of the bodice slide apart.

"How far down do you want me to go?"

When she sucked in a breath, the dress slid from her shoulders and she had to clutch at the front to keep it from sliding completely off.

"That's far enough. Thanks." If it wasn't, she'd cut the dress off herself before she'd ask for more help from him. Without looking back, she grabbed a lantern and bolted awkwardly for the bedroom, nearly tripping on the sagging hem.

Ryan watched her go, the nerves in his fingers still tingling from their contact with her satiny skin, his gaze trapped by the view of partially bared shoulders until the door slammed behind her. Hell's bells, but when Deidre had pointed her out to him in a crush of people, the skimpy strapless number she'd worn then hadn't packed nearly the wallop a flash of skin did just now.

His damn tongue was hanging out.

When he'd impulsively brought her to the cabin, he'd had some crazy idea of presenting her with a business proposition she would immediately see the wisdom in accepting. He hadn't factored in his own reaction to being cooped up alone with her in this isolated setting.

Wanting her wasn't part of the deal!

Once she was safely back in the bedroom with the stout wooden door between them, Sarah leaned back against it and willed her stampeding heartbeat to slow down. What had happened out there?

She might fantasize about a desperado riding into the sunset with her in his arms, but this was real life. Even though the man waiting in the other room looked like a romantic lead didn't mean it would be any less insane for her to fall under his spell.

The door didn't have a lock. With a nervous glance over her shoulder, Sarah stripped off her dress and stepped out of it, stumbling and nearly falling in her haste. Thank goodness she'd decided against the thong underwear the clerk had tried to sell her with the garter belt and matching white lace bra. Sarah had opted instead for high-cut panties, sexy but reasonably comfortable.

Grabbing the T-shirt she'd set out earlier, she pulled it over her head. The hem hit the tops of her thighs. The baggy sweatpants she tugged on threatened to fall down until she tightened the drawstring, but the outfit was wonderfully wearable after the restrictions of her wedding gown.

Unable to leave the garment in such a pathetic heap, she shook out the wrinkles and hung it in Ryan's closet, next to a row of plaid flannel shirts in various stages of deterioration. For a moment self-pity threatened to overwhelm her, as though she were hanging away her dreams along with the dress.

Biting her lip, Sarah shoved the dress to the far end of the row. Briefly she toyed with the idea of layering enough of his shirts to keep her warm during an escape attempt, but without some kind of boots to protect her feet, the idea was an impractical one at best. Tempted as she was to remain hiding in the bedroom, she forced herself to rejoin her captor instead.

The more she found out about him, the more intrigued she became and the more convinced that his intention, although misguided, was genuine. Unless what he'd told her about his background was a total fabrication, it was easy to understand how he might scoff at the idea of a love match. Wouldn't it be something if Sarah, as well as making him see he'd grabbed the wrong bride, was also able to convince him that a marriage without love really was a lot like a day, no, an entire lifetime, without sunshine?

She smiled to herself as she grabbed the lantern and went to find him. Ryan in love, his silvery eyes turned smoky with desire, his face flushed with passion, would certainly be a sight to behold.

Not that she wanted him looking at *her* like that, she reminded herself. It was Jessica who should be the recipient of his devotion, the same woman who had already run out on him once and driven him to this desperate act that had brought Sarah here. So what guarantee was there that she wouldn't hurt him again if he *did* fall for her? Perhaps he was right after all to want something based on a more practical foundation.

Before Sarah could begin to work it out, she found herself in the entrance to the living room where Ryan stood before the fireplace with his back to her. Apparently he hadn't heard her muffled footsteps.

Not wishing to startle him, she cleared her throat. "Am I intruding?" she asked.

He spun around, his gaze sweeping over her. In his hand was a brass poker. "Well, don't you look different?"

Sarah glanced down at her borrowed clothes and thought of the cute pantsuit she'd bought for the trip to Vegas. "Too bad you didn't think to grab my overnight case back at the church."

"We've been through that," he replied. "I'm sorry I don't stock a line of women's wear."

"It's my cosmetics I miss the most," she admitted.

He peered closer. "You certainly don't need makeup to be beautiful."

She had no idea how to handle the compliment. No doubt he was only trying to put her at ease. She knew how she looked. She'd scrubbed her face, but without a little enhancement her eyebrows disappeared and her skin was too pale. Her hair, which had been ruthlessly moussed and smoothed back earlier, needed a good shampooing to restore its normal waves.

Uncomfortable with the intense way he was staring, she looked down at her clasped hands. The manicure she'd been so proud of was surprisingly intact.

"Will you take me home in the morning?" she asked.

Ryan turned away to poke at the fire. His broad shoulders were slumped. "I can't do that."

Sarah was about to argue when she heard something from outside. It sounded like a branch scraping against the front door, except there was no wind.

Apparently Ryan heard it, too, because he crossed the room and listened intently with his ear to the panel. The scraping sound came again and with it this time she heard a low whine.

"Do you have a dog?" she asked, knowing that was unlikely. He wouldn't have left it up here alone.

He shook his head and moved to the window, cupping his hands to block out the light as he peered through the glass. Sarah joined him. Luckily the snow had stopped and the moon had broken through the clouds. There was a trail of paw prints leading up to the front door, where she could see a dark four-legged shape huddled and shivering.

"Oh, the poor thing," she murmured.

Swearing under his breath, Ryan punched a code into the keypad on the wall. Opening the door cautiously, he squatted down on his haunches while Sarah looked over his shoulder. The rush of cold air nearly took her breath away and she was glad she wasn't out in it somewhere trying to thumb a ride back to town.

"It's okay," Ryan crooned gently, extending his hand as Sarah muffled a gasp. "We won't hurt you."

Huddled on the doorstep was a cowering, bedraggled Irish Setter. While Sarah watched, it sniffed Ryan's fingertips and then its tail thumped twice.

"I don't know how people can be so cruel," he said in the same singsong voice as he scratched behind the dog's ears. "Probably someone's dumped it along the main road, not caring if it starves or freezes to death."

"How do you know it's not lost?" Sarah asked quietly so as not to frighten the poor animal. "It could have jumped out of a car or run away." As if the dog understood what was being said, its liquid brown eyes shifted from Ryan to her and back again.

"I doubt that. It doesn't have tags or a collar, even though there's a mark from one in its fur. I suppose there's always a chance the collar fell off or got caught on something, but I'd be willing to bet that whoever left the dog removed it deliberately, so the poor thing couldn't be traced back to them. Right now what it needs is to warm up and be fed. The rest we can deal with later.'' Cautiously he ran his hands over the animal's body as it began to tremble visibly.

"Our new friend is thin," Ryan said. "I can feel its ribs and the fur is all matted. My guess is it's been wandering around in the woods for a few days at least."

Slowly he eased the dog up into his arms and then he straightened as effortlessly as if it didn't weigh a thing. The dog whimpered as though it was in pain, the sound tearing at Sarah's heart, as Ryan's gaze met hers.

"I hope you wouldn't be so foolish as to run off while it's still dark outside," he said somberly after he'd nudged the door shut with his foot. "We're a fair distance from the highway, there's not much traffic and you might not be as lucky as Red here was."

Sarah's mouth dropped open. Taking advantage of the situation hadn't occurred to her.

Ryan watched her as though he was waiting for a reply. The dog, still cradled in his arms, took the opportunity to lick Ryan's cheek.

"Good boy," he murmured absently.

"What do you want from me?" Sarah demanded when he still didn't move.

"Your word that you won't run off," Ryan replied. "Red needs attention and I can't be looking over my shoulder every minute to make sure you're still here."

The dog whined again and began to wiggle, as though it understood Ryan's words and was adding its support.

"Oh, all right," Sarah exclaimed, feeling outnumbered. "But I do have one condition."

Ryan's brows rose in query. "What?" he asked warily.

"I refuse to call the dog Red. We have to come up with something a little more original than that."

His grin was reluctant. "Do you have any suggestions?" he asked as he crossed to the hearth and laid his burden down with care.

Sarah pushed the door shut as the animal gave a contented sigh and stretched out on its side, clearly exhausted. "Something Irish, of course." She thought for a moment while Ryan put a couple more logs on the fire and secured the screen. "It's a boy?"

He glanced up, laughter dancing in his eyes and relaxing the set of his mouth. "No doubt about it."

Heat climbed Sarah's cheeks. "Well, I didn't get a thorough look at him," she blustered.

Now Ryan was openly grinning at her as he straightened. "Want me to turn him over?"

"Of course not!" She took a step backward. For some reason, this new smiling Ryan was ten times as threatening to her peace of mind as he'd been before.

"What can I do to help?" she asked, partly to divert him and partly because she felt so sorry for the dog, who appeared to have fallen instantly asleep.

"His pads are in bad shape. He's traveled a long way and the snow hasn't helped any. I'll clean them up while you find something to feed him. Some soup or broth will do for now. After he's rested we'll give him some canned hash, but I don't want to rush it and make him sick.''

''I don't know how to use the stove,'' Sarah confessed.

Ryan glanced at the dog, completely still except for the slight rise and fall of its stomach. ''Come on, I'll show you while I get some warm water for his feet. Now what have you decided to name him?''

''How about Quincy or MacDuff?'' she suggested as she followed Ryan to the kitchen.

''You know, you may be right,'' he replied over his shoulder. ''It's possible he's got an owner who's looking for him. Perhaps we'd better not give him a name.''

Sarah studied him thoughtfully as he rummaged in the cupboard and came up with a can of beef bouillon. ''Afraid you'd get attached and it would be hard to give him up?'' she guessed.

He gave her a guilty glance as he got out the opener. ''Here, pay attention.'' Ignoring her question, he showed her how to work the propane stove. Then he got out a large pan and filled it from the sink. ''The hot water heater is propane, too,'' he added.

''How convenient,'' Sarah muttered, watching him grab a washcloth.

''There's antiseptic cream in the bathroom medicine cabinet. Would you mind getting that and a couple of bath towels? I don't want him to wake up alone and be frightened.''

Without waiting for her reply, he carried the pan of water back to the living room. Sarah gave the broth a stir and then went to fetch the items he needed. She wasn't doing it for Ryan, she reasoned, but for the dog.

"I'm naming him Quincy," she called out defiantly.

"Much more clever and original than Red," Ryan drawled.

Since she wasn't sure how to take his comment, she ignored it as she laid the towels and the tube of medicine next to him. His touch as he bathed each of Quincy's feet was gentle, and when the dog's head came up in obvious alarm, he murmured a soothing stream of nonsense.

"Do you have children?" Sarah blurted as he dabbed a cut with antibiotic cream.

He glanced up in surprise. "No. Why?"

"Just wondered," she muttered. "I'll go check on the broth."

She lingered for a moment while his hands worked their magic, tenderly drying the damp red hair with a thick cream towel that had to be expensive Egyptian cotton.

"Don't let it get too hot," he called out.

On her way back to the kitchen she noticed the dirty pinkish drips of melting snow and blood marring the finish on the hardwood floor. She didn't want to be impressed with this side of Ryan Noble, but she doubted she'd be able to help it.

By the time they'd fed Quincy and Ryan made up a bed for the dog on old blankets in the corner of the living room, it was late and Ryan was struggling not to yawn. All in all, it had been a stressful day and he was beat.

"We should turn in," he said after he'd reset the alarm. Despite her promise, he wasn't sure she understood just how dangerous sneaking off in the night would be. He was normally a light sleeper, but he wasn't taking any chances with Stuart's granddaughter.

She'd been a big help with the dog, holding its head and stroking its ears while he spooned a little soup into its mouth. After a couple of swallows, Quincy had staggered to his feet and finished the bowl of broth on his own.

The cuts on his paws didn't look bad enough to bandage and Ryan figured he'd only chew bandages off anyway, so after the dog made a quick trip outside to take care of necessities, Ryan applied more antiseptic cream and then patted the folded blanket. After a thorough sniff of the makeshift bed, Quincy circled a couple of times and dropped like a rock. Now he was snoring softly.

Jessica, too, looked tired. The situation was proving to be fraught with more complications than Ryan had first envisioned. He took a deep breath.

"Are you willing to marry me?" he asked.

She'd been watching Quincy, but his question snapped her head around. There were smudges under her eyes and her cheeks were pale, making it impossible for him to ignore the stress she must be feeling.

Her gaze clashed with his. "Don't be ridiculous."

It wasn't the answer he'd hoped for, but was the one he expected. "I had to ask," he said. "We'll talk some more in the morning."

"You won't change my mind."

He ignored her comment. "I'll take the couch so I can keep an eye on the dog," he said. "I want to keep the fire built up so he won't get a chill."

Feeling awkward, he jammed his hands into his hip pockets. "You can count on complete privacy in the bedroom."

She nodded wearily. "Thank you. I hope Quincy will be okay."

"Food and rest is what he needs," Ryan replied. "Go ahead and use the bathroom first. There's enough warm water for a shower if you don't take too long. Just let me know when you're through."

Sarah studied him for a moment, trying to figure him out. Finally she turned away without answering, too tired to deal with the apparent contradictions in his character.

A shower sounded heavenly. She needed to wash the gel from her hair and rinse out her underwear, too, if she expected it clean for the morning. At least the scraps of nylon should dry quickly. Meanwhile another of his T-shirts and a pair of running shorts would serve as pajamas.

She thought of the aqua lace teddy she'd packed for her honeymoon. Flannel long-john pajamas would serve her better here.

When she came back out of the bathroom, swaddled in the dark green velour robe she'd found hanging behind the door and with her freshly shampooed hair wrapped in a towel, Ryan was sitting on the couch staring into the fire. He'd removed his shirt, and his chest gleamed like polished bronze in the firelight. A light dusting of dark hair only added to his masculine image. An unwelcome jolt of attraction shuddered through Sarah as she tried not to stare. It was obvious that he didn't spend all his time behind a desk making deals.

"I lit the woodstove in the bedroom," he said as he got to his feet, his gaze roaming over her. "I hope you found everything you needed."

She drew the edges of the robe together self-consciously, her wet underwear concealed in a tight ball in her other hand. "I made do," she replied, "but I miss having my own things."

A muscle flexed in his cheek. "Unfortunately, there's nothing I can do about that."

Tired as she was, Sarah couldn't let his statement stand unchallenged. "You *choose* to do nothing," she corrected him.

He raked a hand through his hair, drawing her attention to the long muscles of his arm and shoulder. "Dammit," he said, voice rising, "you know the situation as well as I do. If there had been anything I could have done differently, I would have, but you were on the verge of marrying someone else. I had no choice but to stop you any way I could."

"Oh, so now it's my fault?" she retorted angrily.

From his pallet in the corner, Quincy lifted his head

and whined anxiously, his wide eyes rimmed with white.

"Now look what you've done," Sarah snapped. "Maybe you can sweet-talk a dog into trusting you, but don't waste your breath on me. I'm going to bed."

She stalked out, leaving him to calm Quincy the best he could. When she closed the bedroom door behind her, she noticed that in addition to lighting the woodstove, Ryan had left two candles burning in glass holders and had turned down the bed for her, making the room appear downright welcoming.

Annoyed at how difficult staying angry at him was becoming, she hung her bra and panties over the back of a chair near the stove and removed the towel from her head. Bending closer to the heat, she fluffed out her hair so that it would finish drying more quickly.

An image of Ryan trying to fold his long body onto the couch so he could sleep made her smile perversely until she realized that nothing except an unlocked door and a questionable promise kept him from joining her in the bed. Maybe that was what he'd planned all along and he'd only stayed in the other room so she would let down her guard.

Nervously Sarah stared at the door, half expecting it to burst open and reveal him on the threshold, crazed with lust. When the door remained closed, she took a deep breath and willed her thudding heart to return to normal.

Now that the vulnerability of her situation had insinuated itself into her fertile mind, how was she supposed to sleep? Like a cornered rat looking for an escape route, her gaze darted around the room until it finally settled on the other sturdy wooden chair. As quietly as she could, she lugged it over to the door and wedged it firmly beneath the knob. Then she climbed into bed, feeling slightly more secure.

She sank into the mattress with a groan of contentment, not realizing until this moment what a huge toll the events of the day had taken. Sighing, she relaxed for the first time since she'd opened her eyes this morning. How drastically a person's life could change in the course of a few short hours.

Her last conscious thought was that if Ryan slept poorly and woke up feeling stiff and sore, he had no one to blame but himself.

Chapter Four

Ryan slept fitfully, struggling against the temptation to look in on Jessica. Once when he got up to put a log on the fire he actually went to the bedroom door and reached for the knob before sanity regained a foothold and sent him back to the living room.

When he did manage to doze off, his six-foot frame crammed onto the five-foot couch, he dreamed he was standing at the altar, watching her come down the aisle in the same wrinkled wedding dress she'd worn today. The only problem was that after they'd spoken their vows and he lifted the veil hiding her face, he realized it wasn't Jessica he'd married. As he stared, Stuart rushed up and demanded to know why Ryan had let him down.

Ryan came awake from the dream with a start. In the glow from the fire he could see Quincy's head pop up. Scrubbing a hand over his face, Ryan waited for the dog to indicate whether he needed to go outside. Instead his silky head plopped down on his paws. With a drawn-out sigh, the dog went back to sleep, leaving Ryan with only the fire and the darkness for company. Except for Quincy's soft snores and the hoot of an owl, all was quiet. The silence gave Ryan plenty of time to think.

Too damn much time.

He tried to outline his presentation, something sensible and persuasive, but instead his usually well-organized mind kept leading him down alternate—and unwelcome—pathways. Knowing that Jessica slept just beyond the unlocked bedroom door was a powerful distraction. Wondering what, if anything, she'd found to sleep in, caused his thoughts to scatter like post-wedding rice.

Shutting his eyes, he refocused on his strategy, as he would with any business deal he was determined to close in a timely manner. In the morning, over breakfast, he would enumerate the main points of his argument and then deal with Jessica's possible objections one by one until he had obliterated them all. What a damn shame he hadn't thought to bring pie charts, he thought with a self-deprecating snort. Maybe roses would have been more effective, but he was determined to keep romance out of the mix. Emotion was too unreliable for something this important.

Satisfied with his plan, he rolled over with his back

to the fireplace. His legs were bent nearly double and his feet stuck out as he pulled the blanket up over his bare shoulders. He was just about to drift off when he heard Jessica scream.

A terrifying stranger was chasing her through a forest. As she darted between the trees, she kept looking back, but he was hidden in the shadows. The trees grew closer and closer together, until finally she had nowhere left to run. Cornered and desperate, she turned to face her pursuer as a heavy cloak was thrown over her head, smothering her. With a last burst of effort, she fought her way free of the confining folds, sucked in a breath and screamed.

Sarah's eyes flew open and she stared at the shadowy log walls, her heart pounding like a car stereo with the bass cranked up. The cabin wasn't part of her nightmare; it was all too real.

Something crashed against the door and the knob rattled, but the chair she'd propped against it held as she sat huddled in the middle of the bed in the dark with the covers pulled up to her nose.

"Jessica! Are you all right?" shouted a familiar male voice as the wooden panel shook from another blow. "What the hell is wrong with this door?"

Pressing the edge of the quilt against her mouth to keep herself from screaming again, she peered into the darkness as full awareness returned with a rush.

"Jessica!" This time there was an edge of panic in the deep voice.

Releasing her death grip on the quilt, Sarah scrambled from the bed. "Just a minute," she called as a blast of cold air hit her bare legs.

The doorknob rattled again. "Let me in!"

"Okay, okay," she muttered, groping for the matches. "Keep your knickers on. I'm coming."

As she lit the candle, another thud hit the door, followed by a string of swear words that made her eyes widen. She was tempted to leave the chair where it was, but a shattered door would give her even less privacy than she had now.

"I'm opening it," she shouted when the swearing subsided.

The last thing she wanted was for him to come crashing into her. The second she removed the chair, the door flew open to reveal Ryan, his eyes wild, his powerful muscles flexed and his hands doubled into fists. He practically bristled with testosterone as he looked from her to the chair and back again.

"You screamed," he said, as if that explained everything.

"I had a nightmare," she admitted breathlessly, suppressing a shiver of purely feminine reaction as she forced herself to turn away from the sight of his broad chest. "I'm sorry if I alarmed you." What was she doing apologizing to him? It was his fault she was here.

He was silent except for the sound of his breathing. A match flared as he lit a second candle. When Sarah looked up, he was rubbing his shoulder, his gaze sliding down her bare legs and back to her face.

Resisting the urge to tug down the hem of her borrowed T-shirt, she folded her arms across her chest and returned his stare, doing her best to ignore her reaction to his sudden appearance.

"Are you okay?" he asked, rotating his shoulder with care. The skin appeared to be scraped from contact with the door.

"I'm fine. What about you?"

His face took on the stoic expression men wore when they were embarrassed to admit they'd done some minor injury to themselves. "No problem." He sent the chair an accusing glance. "You didn't need to do that." He managed to sound as if his feelings had been hurt.

Ignoring his last comment, Sarah grabbed his arm to hold it still so she could examine the scrapes. His skin was hot to the touch. "The skin is broken. It needs attention."

He pulled free of her grasp, twisting so he could see the injured area in question. "It'll be fine."

"You should probably ice it, too," she continued as if he hadn't spoken. "You must have bruised the muscle, using it like a battering ram the way you were. It will be sore in the morning."

"I was worried about you." His tone sounded downright sulky.

"No, you were feeling guilty," she contradicted. "If anything happens to me, it's on your head."

For a moment they stared at each other mutely. Ryan was the first one to look away, spearing his fingers through his hair. His chest heaved as he sighed.

"I know you don't believe me, but if I could have done this differently—" he began.

"Oh, spare me. For starters you could have snatched the right bride," Sarah snapped back at him, her patience run out. "Now I'm tired. If you don't mind, and even if you do, I'd like to get a little more sleep before I have to face tomorrow's ordeal."

"Is that what I am, an ordeal?"

She ignored the curve of his full lower lip when he pouted. "You got it."

He held her gaze for a moment and then he turned his attention to the woodstove. "Warm enough?" he asked as though they were having an ordinary conversation under ordinary circumstances.

"I was." The air in the room was chilly, but under the covers she'd been fine.

She watched as he added a couple of small logs to the fire.

"That should get you through until morning." He lifted his brow. "Unless you'd like me to stay."

"Couch too short?" she taunted, knowing full well the answer.

"That, too." His tone was dry, but his eyes were dark and hot.

Sarah was about to make another cutting remark when prudence elbowed her. No good could come of further provocation, so she pressed her lips together instead and lifted her chin.

"I'll take that as a no." His gaze cooled, his tone becoming disgruntled.

As she waited for him to leave, relief surged

through Sarah, mingled with a whisper of something else she couldn't identify. A movement caught her eye and she saw Quincy hovering uncertainly in the doorway. She'd nearly forgotten about him.

Bending down, she extended her hand and called him softly. Tail wagging like a burgundy feather, he brushed past Ryan and approached her until he was close enough to sniff her fingers.

"How's he doing?" she asked Ryan as she scratched behind the dog's ears.

"Fine, I think. Although one more night in the woods might have changed things dramatically. The temperature's dropped some."

Sarah continued to stroke Quincy's head and ears. "You're a lucky boy," she crooned.

"He probably needs to go out again," Ryan said. "If you want to climb into your big lonely bed, I'll blow out the candle." His gaze strayed to the chair she'd used to block the door.

"No, thanks. I can find my way after you're gone."

He shrugged. "Whatever."

When he left, the dog looked at him and then back at Sarah. Quincy's company would be reassuring, she thought, but before she could call him, he padded after Ryan, who shut the door behind them without another word.

Standing close to the woodstove, Sarah debated using the chair again, wavered and then reminded herself that just because he was kind to animals didn't mean she could trust her kidnapper not to decide he was entitled to share her bed.

Ryan was standing outside the door when he heard the scrape of the chair. Disheartened by her stubbornness, he headed back to the living room and the inadequate couch with Quincy close on his heels.

If she wouldn't lower her guard and meet him partway, how was he going to persuade her to go along with her grandfather's wishes in the few days he had left? At this point, he hadn't a clue.

The question still taunted him when the sky outside began to lighten and Quincy went over to whine at the door. Ignoring the ache in his shoulder, Ryan checked the dog's feet, pleased to see that the cuts on his pads didn't appear to be infected. Then Ryan pulled on his shirt, shut off the alarm and opened the door. He blinked against the cold as Quincy bolted past him, stopping only a few feet away to relieve himself in a patch of snow.

The wood supply was dwindling, so Ryan went back inside to unlock the closet and pull out his boots, gloves and a faded parka. The snow crunched beneath his feet and the cold air found every sliver of exposed skin as he walked back and forth from the shed carrying armloads of wood into the cabin.

Quincy circled him like a drunken butterfly, barking sharply, his breath vaporizing in the cold. Finally Ryan stopped to toss a stick that Quincy promptly retrieved.

"That's enough," Ryan had to tell him after several more throws. "I've got chores and I don't want you overdoing it."

As if he understood every word, Quincy dropped

the stick and began investigating the underbrush as Ryan went back to the shed for another load of wood. Overhead the sky was clear and colorless, but he knew how quickly the weather could change in the mountains. It wasn't too late in the year for more snow. They had enough food, propane and wood to outlast any storm. What they didn't have was time.

He should call Stuart with an update before Jessica got up, he realized grimly as he shed his outerwear and returned it to the closet. The old man was an early riser and he'd be wondering about Ryan's progress. Since there was nothing to report, he left the cell phone locked in his briefcase and headed for the kitchen to make coffee and find something to feed Quincy.

Ryan had opened a can of hash for the dog and was about to take a shower when he realized all his clean clothes were in the bedroom with Jessica. Before he could decide what to do while he waited, he heard her coming down the hall.

"Good morning." He forced a smile she didn't bother to return.

"It will be if you agree to take me home today," she replied as she bent to pat Quincy's head.

She was wearing another pair of his sweats with a different T-shirt, a blue one that matched the color of her eyes, and her hair was fluffed out around her face as if she'd run her fingers through it. The faded football logo on the front of the T-shirt had never looked as good on him as it did hinting at the curves it hid, even though the shirt was miles too big, but he didn't figure she'd appreciate his pointing that out.

"Coffee's made," he said instead.

Nodding silently, she brushed by. "You want some?" she asked, surprising him.

"Sure, thanks." Where to begin? Now that the time had come, he found himself strangely reluctant to resume his argument that she marry him and make her grandfather a happy man.

"Let's take a walk after breakfast," he suggested impulsively as she got two mugs from the cupboard and filled them.

Enthusiasm lit up her features before she managed to mask it. Was she thinking of escape or merely fresh air? "There seems to be an absence of warm clothing and boots," she said dryly.

Ryan felt the heat climb his cheeks. "I can find some, if you're interested.

She shrugged. "Okay. How's your shoulder?"

He raised his arm, refusing to wince or to admit it was tender. "Just fine."

She gave him a knowing look, but didn't comment.

After he'd showered and changed, he cooked ham and eggs for their breakfast. She poured orange juice and set the table, the two of them moving around each other easily, as if they'd been doing it for years. They could adapt to each other, if she'd only try.

"Do you like to cook?" she asked as he turned the eggs without breaking the yokes.

"I like to eat," he replied. "When I was a kid my

mother was always working, so I had to fix supper for my sisters and me.''

She was watching him intently, so he cleared his throat and went on. ''I put myself through college slinging hash at a local hangout, so I guess it paid off.'' Expertly he slid the food onto two plates.

Hell, he was worth a fortune and here he was showing off his short-order skills. What a way to impress a woman like Jessica, whose experience in the kitchen until now had probably been limited to interaction with the staff.

''You're certainly a man of many talents.''

Wondering just how she'd meant that last remark, Ryan brought the plates to the table and then he pulled out her chair. His mother had drilled good manners into him when she was around, which hadn't been often.

''Thank you,'' Jessica murmured as he sat down across from her and spread his napkin on his lap.

As they started eating, Ryan was trying to figure out his weird compulsion to tell her about his past. None of his acquaintances were even aware that he'd worked his way through school.

''I gather you've come a long way since then,'' she said after she'd sampled the eggs. ''Just from seeing this cabin, I can guess you've reached some level of financial success.'' She cut a piece of ham. ''I'm sure you don't need to marry someone for their money.'' Her gaze darted to his and then away again. ''You should follow your heart, not your wallet,'' she concluded.

"Like you were going to do?" he asked.

"We're not talking about me," she replied a little too quickly, "but I certainly wasn't marrying Dan for his money."

"Maybe he was marrying you for yours," Ryan suggested.

She rolled her eyes. "Right. He was after the big salary I pull down at the bank."

"So you really do work there?" Ryan asked. It made sense that she would have some kind of job to support herself since she'd run off. She hadn't been drawing on the Walker family funds while she was incognito.

"Give the man a gold star," she muttered.

Ryan figured there was no point in pushing the discussion about her former fiancé. Besides, Ryan didn't consider the other man much of an obstacle, not after what she'd let slip.

Sarah was surprised that he didn't pursue the conversation. Was it possible he was starting to believe her, or at least to have a few doubts that she really was Jessica Walker?

As they continued with their meal, she thought about the glimpse Ryan had given her into a childhood she suspected he didn't discuss very often. The simple fact that he didn't try to use it to gain her sympathy impressed her.

How could she be attracted to a man who didn't even know who she was? The whole thing was insane.

As soon as they were done eating, Ryan cleared the table. "Ready for that walk?" he asked.

Perhaps once they were outside, she could come up with an escape plan, even though the more time she spent with him the less wary and more curious she became. If he'd intended to force her into anything, last night would have been the perfect opportunity, and yet he'd left her alone. They couldn't stay here forever, and she wasn't eager to face the mess back in Bellville. Perhaps waiting him out would be the most sensible course of action after all.

"I'd love to go outside," she replied.

Moments later she watched silently while he unlocked the closet door with a key from his pocket. She'd been right about its contents.

"You've got small feet," he said, "but these might work with a couple more pairs of thick socks." He handed her some thermal boots that looked gigantic as well as a heavy jacket, gloves and a knit cap from the supply in the closet.

"What about Quincy?" she asked as the dog circled them excitedly. Apparently he knew what the donning of jackets signified. "Won't he get chilled?"

"Naw, it's not that cold and we won't be gone long. I'll get you some boot socks."

Ryan's shoulders looked impossibly broad in a worn black parka. From the clothes she'd seen him wear so far, she wouldn't have guessed he was a successful businessman, but there were plenty of other hints, from the confident way he carried himself to the shape his hands were in. Although they looked strong and tanned, the nails were clean and neatly trimmed.

At the bank where she worked, she was seldom wrong about which customers were successful and which ones merely dressed the part. A person's clothing could be misleading, but not the manner in which it was worn.

It wasn't the balance in a man's bank account that appealed to her. What she found attractive was the self-assurance that came from knowing who you were.

It was something Sarah hadn't yet figured out about herself.

Ryan came back and handed her some heavy socks. ''These should do the trick.''

The whiskers darkening his cheeks gave him a rakish appearance Sarah was annoyed to realize she found way too appealing. When her gaze met his, he smiled. It seemed so genuine that she found herself returning it before she could stop herself.

She took the socks with a mumbled thanks. How she wished they were two ordinary people going for a walk together with their dog, she thought while she donned the sheepskin-lined jacket she suspected was what he usually wore instead of the old parka.

During the winter, Dan had taken her sledding with his sister and a friend of Kelly's from work. It had been fun, partly because of the other couple's nonstop teasing, and partly because they'd all gone by Dan's parents' house afterwards for cocoa and freshly baked cookies.

Sarah still remembered the warmth and the good smells in the old-fashioned kitchen where they all sat around the table. Until her talk with Ryan this morning, she hadn't given Dan a thought.

What must the poor man be going through, assuming she'd run out on him? And what did his parents think of her now? When she got back to Bellville, would she be able to mend the damage her disappearance had caused, or would the rift be too wide?

If she was entirely honest with herself, she would have to admit that one of Dan's greatest attractions for her had been his close, warmhearted family. Spending time with them gave her a sense of belonging she hadn't felt since her parents had died. How she dreaded losing that again.

"Ready?" Ryan asked, bringing her back to the present.

Perhaps some fresh air and exercise would curb Sarah's jangling nerves so she could come up with a way out of this mess. "Sure." She clumped past him in the too-large boots and then waited while he reset the alarm. She tried to get a peek at the code, but either accidentally or on purpose, his shoulder blocked her view.

"Which way?" she asked, looking around. Quincy had run in a big circle with his nose to the ground, leaving a ring of footprints in the snow, and now he was waiting impatiently for them with his breath clouding the air.

The narrow road they'd come up ended at the cabin, but a path continued on from where the Jeep was parked and wound its way through the trees before it eventually disappeared. Ryan pointed in that direction.

"I'd rather be walking downhill on the return trip," he said. "How about you?"

Short of hiking to the main road and flagging down a car, Sarah had no preference. With a shrug, she started slogging awkwardly through the snow in the oversized boots. He wouldn't have to worry about her trying to run away in these. They felt as big on her feet as snowshoes, just not as efficient. For a little while, they hiked in silence as the path gradually grew steeper.

"Is there anything around here but woods?" she asked innocently, stopping to catch her breath.

"The nearest cabins are at least ten miles away," Ryan replied. "I wouldn't advise trying to reach any of them on foot."

Being read so easily was annoying. "Especially barefoot," she snapped back. "I'm sure you're planning to lock the footwear up again the minute we get back."

"I've only done what I have to." His tone was infuriatingly reasonable.

How could she be attracted to him one minute and ready to wring his neck the next? "You don't believe that any more than I do," she couldn't resist pointing out. He'd *admitted* he had panicked and acted on impulse.

He drew up beside her, his cheeks red from the

cold air and his eyes a dark, stormy gray. "All you have to do is agree to marry me," he pointed out.

"In a heartbeat, if it means we can leave."

"Seal it with a kiss?" he asked, leaning toward her.

Sarah backed up so quickly she nearly lost her balance.

He cocked his head to one side as he continued to study her. "Gee, why don't I believe you?" he mused aloud.

Sarah slapped her forehead with her gloved hand. "Oh, I don't know. Maybe you're starting to realize what a dumb idea this was."

His mouth tightened. "Maybe so, but I'm afraid we're stuck with it." He started to move past her when she grabbed his arm.

"Why are you so determined to do what your business partner wants?" she demanded. "What about what *you* want? We don't even know each other. You can't be crazy about marrying a stranger."

"You're not a stranger," he insisted. "I know a lot about you. Deidre told me."

"Deidre being my mother?" Sarah asked with a sneer.

He shook off her hold on his arm. "We could make it work."

"Not without love," she insisted as he trudged on ahead.

"You were willing to marry without it before," he tossed back over his shoulder.

Sarah opened her mouth, but the words wouldn't come out. Would she have come to love Dan the way a woman should love her husband? She didn't know the answer to that anymore. Certainly she'd never felt the mixture of exasperation and attraction this man provoked in her.

Was this the Stockholm Syndrome she'd heard about, when prisoners started to confuse their feelings toward their captors, on whom they were dependent for everything? Was she imagining the flashes of vulnerability she glimpsed in him or had she read too many pirate stories growing up in which the heroine always fell for the masterful yet misunderstood captain? Either way, Sarah needed to remember *she* wasn't the one Ryan wanted, although she was certainly curious to meet the woman he'd mistaken her for.

The woman Ryan Noble was willing to break the law to win.

Chapter Five

"Has he called yet?" Deidre Walker asked her father-in-law as she stood in the doorway of his richly appointed den.

Stuart looked up from the papers spread across the top of his massive antique desk, a frown deepening the lines etched into his face by time and the dry Nevada air. "No. It's only been fifteen minutes since you asked me that."

Deidre resisted the uncharacteristic urge to fidget. After more than twenty years, the old man still intimidated her and she resented him for it. "I just want to know that Jessica is all right," she replied, letting the tears well up in her eyes. Tears had always worked with her late husband, Lawrence, and they had the same effect on his father.

Stuart set aside his reading glasses and got to his feet, moving easily for a man of seventy-five. He crossed the room to give Deidre a reassuring hug. For a moment she allowed herself to melt into his arms, but then he released her and stepped back.

Despite the fact that she and Jessica had lived with him since Lawrence's unexpected death more than two decades ago and Deidre had never remarried, there was an invisible line that Stuart had never once crossed. How much easier strengthening her position within the family would have been if the old man had ever allowed himself to loosen up.

She looked up at him through her lashes and managed a tremulous smile. "Do you think Jessica is safe, alone with him in that cabin?" she asked.

She'd been livid last night when Stuart informed her that Ryan had called while she was attending a dinner party at Kikki Van Damm's. The young fool was supposed to bring Jessica straight back home where Deidre could keep an eye on them both, not whisk her away to some rustic bachelor retreat for a weekend of who knew what.

Deidre's plan to marry her daughter to Stuart's favorite business associate and thus maintain her own influential position in the Walker empire had taken an unexpected turn when Jessica exhibited an uncharacteristic streak of rebellion and ran away. The girl had no idea how difficult it was to claw one's way up the social ladder. Thanks to Deidre's efforts, Jessica had lived a life of privilege, never wanting for anything. Now it was her turn to repay Deidre by doing what was expected of her.

"I trust Ryan," Stuart replied gruffly as he returned to his leather executive chair.

He'd aged in the time Jessica had been gone, Deidre realized. When his granddaughter was small, he'd been too busy building a financial empire to pay her much attention. Now that he was considering retirement, he was determined to turn over both his business and his only heir to his own hand-picked successor.

"He's a man," she replied with a sneer. Even her own husband had been a chaser before he died, and she had no doubt that a handsome young stud like Ryan Noble wasn't any different. It didn't stop Deidre for a moment from doing everything she could to see that he married her daughter. Stuart wanted it, and pleasing Stuart was Deidre's first priority. As much as she loved Jessica, she would have to admit that she loved the lifestyle she enjoyed as Lawrence Walker's widow even more.

What Deidre didn't like was not knowing what was happening in that cabin. Jessica's recent refusal to go along with Deidre's matchmaking plans had been disconcerting, to say the least. She'd better not be messing up the second chance she'd been handed when Ryan's investigator spotted her photo in that small-town rag. How *dare* Jessica get herself engaged to some nobody just to spite her family, especially when they had her best interests at heart!

Deidre had no idea where her daughter's sudden

streak of defiance had come from, unless it was some throwback to the girl's birth mother. Who knew what kind of unsavory genes Larissa Summers, one of Lawrence's low-class playmates, might have passed on to her baby!

"Stop worrying," Stuart said as he flipped open another folder. "I've known Ryan for a long time. He's an honorable man and he's not going to take advantage of Jessica. All he wants is a few days to win her over, and he could hardly do that with us watching them like a pair of mother hens, now could he? Why don't you run along and I'll let you know the moment I hear from him."

Without looking at her again, Stuart began keying information into his computer, and Deidre knew she'd been dismissed. "Thank you," she murmured through gritted teeth. Head held high, she left the room, the tapping of her heels on the polished hardwood the only outward sign of her annoyance that she allowed herself.

Someday Stuart's health was bound to falter and then their positions would be reversed, she vowed. He would be helpless and *she* would be in charge. When that day came, she would make the old man pay for every time he'd slighted her. Until then, she would bide her time and hope to hell that Jessica had finally come to her senses and accepted Ryan's proposal.

"For the last time, I'm not Jessica Walker and I refuse to marry someone who can't use my real name!'' Sarah ignored the hand Ryan extended, managing to scramble over the fallen log without his assistance.

She shot him a triumphant glance over her shoulder as she reached the other side, but when she took another step in the oversized boots, her feet shot out from under her and she landed hard on her bottom on a patch of ice. Her teeth snapped together, nearly severing the tip of her tongue, as Ryan leaped over the log and bent down to peer at her.

''Did you hurt anything?'' he demanded as Quincy pushed his way to her side, whining anxiously.

Sarah let out a disgusted sigh and glared up at Ryan. ''Well, I didn't land on my head, did I?''

Humor sparked in his eyes, but he wisely squelched it as he stuck out his gloved hand. ''May I help you up?'' he asked, his voice not quite steady.

Sarah debated ignoring his offer just as she was trying to ignore the smothered laughter in his voice, but then she figured that one fall onto the hard, frozen ground was more than enough for the day and for her poor bottom. She grabbed his glove as impersonally as though it were a tree branch and allowed him to pull her to her feet.

''Okay?'' he asked when she was upright.

Sarah nodded, refusing to meet his gaze. As she dusted the snow from her sweatpants, he glanced up at the sky.

''It looks as though we're in for a storm,'' he said. ''Perhaps we'd better head back.''

''Fine with me.'' She glanced at the fallen log and

decided to be sensible. "Would you mind helping me?"

"Sure thing." Instead of sticking out his hand again, Ryan clasped her waist. Before she could ask just what he thought he was doing, she was airborne.

Her squeak of protest snagged in her throat when he set her down on the other side of the log as easily as if she weighed no more than Quincy. When she grabbed a branch to steady herself and turned to glare at his high-handed treatment, he gave her a cocky grin she would have paid quite a bit to wipe from his smug face. Instead she stuck out her chin, called to the dog and started down the trail without waiting for her irritating companion to join her.

Before she took half a dozen shuffling steps, a snowball caught her in the back of the head and slid down inside the collar of her borrowed parka.

Gasping at the icy-cold invasion, she grabbed at her neck with her gloved hand, only succeeding in pushing the snow farther down inside her jacket, directly onto her bare skin. She whirled around to see Ryan doubled over helplessly, his cheeks red as he whooped with laughter, his breath turning to cloudy puffs in the cold air.

Little did he know that Sarah had been the star pitcher on her girls' softball team. Scooping up a handful of snow, she fashioned it into a firm ball and fired it at his head.

He glanced up as the snowball found its target and took it full in the face. As he stood sputtering and wiping the snow from his eyes, it was Sarah's turn to laugh.

"Where'd you learn to throw like that?" he demanded, slapping his baseball cap against his thigh to dislodge the rest of the snow.

"Didn't you know about my athletic career?" she demanded.

He looked puzzled. "Horseback riding, tennis and golf," he recited.

She shook her head, correcting him. "Softball and soccer. You're lucky I didn't kick you in the shins while you were temporarily blinded."

His puzzlement was replaced by a wide grin. "Lucky shot," he replied. "But you did have me going for a minute there."

"Lucky shot!" she echoed, offended. "I'll show you lucky, you arrogant idiot." She grabbed more snow and fired off another missile, but this time she rushed it and the snowball sailed harmlessly past his ear.

With a wink that infuriated her, he cleared the log and advanced on her as she reached for more ammunition. Again she threw too quickly as he ducked out of the way. His laughter floated around her as he fired. In her haste to avoid being hit, she lost her footing. The loosely packed snowball still managed to knock off her hat and shower her with the cold wet stuff before she went down face first.

Silently admitting defeat, she rolled over so she was looking up at Ryan as he towered over her. Quincy swiped his tongue across her face before Ryan grabbed him by the scruff of the neck and pulled him away from her.

"Give up?" Ryan asked, hands braced on his knees as he surveyed her with an arrogance that set her teeth on edge.

"I'm not sure," she wheezed faintly.

Immediately the triumph on his face changed to concern. "What's wrong?"

"I don't know," she said on a groan. "If you'd just help me up—"

"Here, take it easy." Feet planted on either side of her legs, he bent way down and reached for her shoulders. His face was inches away from hers, his eyes dark with worry. "I'll just—"

Sarah brought up both hands, heaped with snow, and slapped them on either side of his head. As he straightened abruptly with a satisfying grunt, she flipped over and scrambled away from him on her hands and knees.

"Why, you little brat!" he exclaimed as Quincy barked excitedly, adding to the confusion.

Before Sarah could stumble to her feet in the clumsy boots she felt an icy hand duck under the hem of her jacket to grip the loose waist of her sweatpants. "You wouldn't!" she shrieked.

"On, no?"

She froze in place. If she moved, she was in danger of losing her britches. If she stayed where she was, she might end up with snow down them.

Before she could decide what to do, Ryan tackled her, wrapping his arms around her and twisting as they went down so he landed beneath her and his weight didn't crush her.

Lying on top of him, Sarah was instantly aware that their bodies were pressed together from chest to knees. Almost immediately after came the realization that his face was very close to hers. His eyes were hooded, his cheeks flushed and his lips slightly parted. She could see each individual eyelash. She could feel his heart thudding, or was it her own? She wasn't sure; she only knew if she didn't move away right this second, she was apt to do something really stupid.

Before she could lever herself off him, his hand came up to cradle the back of her head and his gaze shifted to her mouth. They were both breathing hard. The stress of the last day and a half transformed itself to raw desire that coiled inside Sarah like a spring about to snap.

She was yielding to the pressure of his hand on the back of her head, urging her closer, her eyes drifting shut, when he spoke.

"Jessica," he groaned raggedly, shattering the spell like broken glass.

For one heartbeat she was so close that Ryan could feel her breath on his face, her eyes dark with desire and her body sinking into his—and the next she was fighting him like an opponent in the wrestling ring on cable television. She pushed hard against his sore shoulder. The elbow she jammed into his ribs in her attempt to get away caught him off guard and drove most of the air from his lungs.

"Hey!" he yelped as her knee nearly did him in. "What the hell is wrong with you?"

"You're what's wrong!" she cried, scrambling to her feet and backing away as though she was terrified.

Ryan stood up, hands held wide in a gesture of submission and reassurance. "I'm sorry. I thought you were willing, or I never would have touched you." How had things gotten so out of hand so quickly? "I'm sorry," he repeated even more earnestly, the realization dawning that she might have felt pressured to go along with him. "You don't have to do anything you don't want to." The idea of coerced sex made his stomach heave and he swallowed hard.

"You called me Jessica," she nearly spat at him. "How could you?"

Ryan's mouth fell open. "Uh, because that's your name."

She grabbed the hat that had somehow fallen off in their scuffle, jammed it back on her head and started marching back toward the cabin without another word. Under different circumstances, her awkward progress might have been funny.

Catching up with her, Ryan grabbed her shoulder, intending only to make sure she understood what he'd been trying to say.

To his surprise, when she spun around, tears were running down her cheeks and her nose was red. He snatched his hand away as though she'd singed his fingers.

"What is it? Why are you crying?" He hated tears. He'd rather have her royally ticked off than upset.

She only shook her head silently as she started walking again. At a loss, he trailed along after her, Quincy at his side. He was getting nowhere and he still had to call Stuart with a progress report.

A few flakes of snow drifted down in front of him, turning his attention to the sky overhead. While they'd been romping like carefree kids, the clouds had turned dark and heavy. Just what they needed.

In just a few minutes of walking, the size and number of the flakes had increased at a rate that made Ryan nervous. The path was easy to follow, but he was no daredevil when it came to Mother Nature, and the last thing he wanted was to put Stuart's granddaughter at risk.

He was concentrating so hard on what he needed to do that he plowed into her, nearly knocking her down because he'd failed to notice she'd stopped dead in the path.

"What's the matter?" he asked as he grabbed her shoulders to keep her from falling.

"It's coming down hard," she replied with a worried frown. "Are we going to get lost?"

He wanted to give her a reassuring hug, but instead he let his hands drop to his sides. "No, of course not. The cabin isn't far, another five minutes. As long as we keep heading downhill, we'll be fine. It's too big to miss, even in this." He hoped he was right.

Her expression cleared and he was gratified that she

believed him. "We've got plenty of food and fuel," he added. "Don't worry."

"What if we get snowed in?"

Mentally Ryan kicked himself. He should have been listening to the weather report on the radio, but he'd assumed it was too late in the season for an extended storm.

"It won't last," he replied breezily. "By tomorrow the temperature will warm up and the snow will start to melt. Now we'd better keep moving, just to be on the safe side."

Obediently she started walking again, the dog plodding along at her side, while Ryan thought of the tire chains sitting back in his garage next to his skis and the snowmobile he'd hauled down there just a couple of weeks ago.

It took longer than his five-minute estimate to get back to the cabin. "I turned on the water heater," he said after they'd removed their jackets and boots. "Why don't you take a warm shower and get into some dry clothes while I towel Quincy off? When you come out I'll fix some cocoa." The dog had gotten covered with snow and now it was melting, leaving puddles on the floor.

Jessica's face was red and the ends of her hair dripped on her T-shirt, soaking her shoulders. "Okay," she agreed. "I'll just be a few minutes."

After she'd left the room, Ryan built up the fire and dried off the dog the best he could. Then he got out his cell phone and tried to call Stuart, but he couldn't get through. The signal from up here in the mountains could be unreliable and the weather probably wasn't helping. He'd have to try again later. Meanwhile he walked to the window and watched the snow. It looked as though they'd be stuck inside for the rest of the day.

By the time Jessica reappeared he'd fed Quincy, who was asleep on the hearth, toweled and combed his own damp hair and was heating canned chili to go with the hot chocolate he'd promised her.

"Feel better?" he asked.

Jessica nodded. Her hair hung in damp waves around her face and her cheeks were still ruddy. Her blue eyes and sooty lashes were in direct contrast to her soft pink lips. Ryan remembered how close he'd come to tasting them and his body tightened with unexpected fervor.

Disconcerted by the strength of his reaction, he turned away abruptly and began dishing up lunch. He wondered how she felt about the incident now that a little time had passed. Had she dismissed it as momentary madness, or did it still stick in her mind as it did his? Throughout the nearly silent meal, he couldn't help but relive those moments when her body had covered him like a sensual blanket and they'd nearly exchanged a kiss.

"Aren't you hungry?" she asked, the sound of her voice jerking his attention to her face. She pointed at his bowl with her spoon. "You aren't eating."

"Just waiting for it to cool a little," he replied gruffly, taking a healthy mouthful that singed his tongue.

She watched him with a concerned expression. "You're worried about the snow, aren't you?"

How could he admit he was more concerned about their being cooped up here together? He didn't want to make her nervous, but now that the lid of Pandora's Box had been opened, it was going to be pretty tough for him to slam it shut again and pretend nothing had happened between them. As it was, he couldn't help but notice the way her mouth moved each time she spoke and wonder if her full lips were as satiny and yielding as they appeared.

"The snow will stop soon," he said with confidence. "Meanwhile we have everything we need right here in the cabin."

Sarah tore her gaze away from his face, absently stirring her chili. Was he as immune to her as he seemed, or was he only pretending? She'd felt his reaction when she'd been sprawled on top of him. It was one that men couldn't hide and it hadn't been to his precious Jessica. Now the question tormenting her was whether his arousal had been merely a knee-jerk male response to the proximity of a female of the species, or was it her, Sarah Daniels, who had provoked it.

It certainly wasn't something she could ask about. With a sigh she took a swallow of her hot chocolate. He'd sprinkled the top with little marshmallows, just the way her mother used to. Peering at him over the rim of her mug, she wondered where he'd learned the homey touch.

"Tell me about your business," she suggested as

the silence between them lengthened. "How did you get started?" Maybe if she understood what drove him, she could find the key to unlock the emotions he seemed to guard so carefully and persuade him to let her go.

Was that what she really wanted? As he set aside his empty bowl with a considering frown, she realized with a little start that the longer she was around him, the more he intrigued her and the less desire she had to leave.

Close on the heels of that shocking revelation followed another. He still believed she was Jessica Walker, the woman he was determined to marry. If Sarah wanted to get closer to him, she would have to do it as Jessica, and quit trying to convince him she was someone else, an insignificant small-town bank employee who could never hope to attract the interest of a man like Ryan Noble.

"My business is too complex to explain without boring you to death," he said gruffly as he pushed back his chair and got to his feet. "Why don't you tell me about your volunteer work instead?" Was he waiting for her to insist yet again that she knew nothing about the details of Jessica's life?

"Why don't we talk about something you *don't* know about me," she suggested daringly. She got up and began helping to clear off the table as calmly as if she hadn't just taken an irreversible step.

"Like what?"

"Like what books I read and what movies I enjoy, for starters." She met his wary gaze squarely, her heart pounding so hard she surprised the vibration wasn't rattling her teeth. "And then you can tell me what you do for fun."

If he was aware of the concession she'd just made, he gave no sign. He merely shrugged. "If fun is what you want to discuss, it's fine with me."

He shifted unexpectedly as Sarah was walking near him and nearly managed to knock the dishes from her hands. As she did her best not to drop them, he reached out to steady her. His warm fingers curled around her forearms and his hooded gaze locked on hers. A frown pleated his forehead and a muscle jumped along his jaw.

"Okay?" he asked hoarsely.

If her hands hadn't been full, she might have pressed a finger to his mouth to test its firmness. Instead she managed to bob her head. "Uh-huh."

Releasing her arms, he lifted his hand to cup her chin while his smokey gaze searched hers. "Don't be afraid of me. Remember that nothing's going to happen that you don't want," he whispered hoarsely. "That's a promise."

"Okay." She couldn't move, could barely breathe.

His eyes had narrowed, darkened, and she felt as though she were drowning in their depths. She was barely aware of his fingers tightening on her chin before he let go. The last shreds of her self-preservation made her take a step back. She was gripping the lunch dishes so tightly that her fingers began to cramp.

Ryan spun away suddenly, shattering the tension between them, and muttered something that she didn't catch. Sarah blinked and let out the breath she'd forgotten she was holding. What was she trying to accomplish here, anyway?

Before she threw herself at him again, she'd better decide whether she really wanted to go through with this little charade. Once she embarked on this particular road, turning back might be more difficult than she could imagine.

Before she could think of anything to say, Quincy whined sharply. He was standing by the door, dancing with anxiety. His imploring brown eyes were fixed on the two humans.

"Saved from the sublime by the mundane," Ryan muttered. "You want to let him out while I do the dishes?"

"Aren't you afraid I'll run off?" she asked.

He glanced at the window, through which they could both see the snow falling heavily. "You're not that stupid."

As a compliment it wasn't much, she thought as she opened the door. The dog rushed out and then skidded to a stop by a snow-covered bush to relieve himself.

It wasn't until Quincy was back inside, shaking loose snow all over Sarah's legs, that she remembered the alarm. It hadn't gone off, which meant that Ryan hadn't reset it when they came back from their walk.

It wasn't as though she could go anywhere. Already their tracks were nearly obliterated.

After she'd dealt with Quincy, she glanced at the cabin's other resident. He was standing at the sink with an apron tied around his middle, doing the dishes and still managing to look more masculine than any man she had ever seen. His head came up and he caught her staring before she could turn away. Something crackled between them, and then Quincy shoved his cold nose into Sarah's hand, startling her.

Leaving Ryan to finish the KP alone, she wandered restlessly into the living room. The fire was burning low, so she added a log. Then she folded the blanket Ryan had left on the couch and sat down.

She was still sitting there, apparently mesmerized by the flames, when Ryan joined her a few minutes later. He wanted to ask what she was thinking, but they hadn't reached that level of familiarity yet. He sat next to her on the couch, leaving a few safe inches between them, and studied her profile.

"So who's your favorite actor?" he asked after he'd cleared his throat with a touch of self-consciousness. He felt not unlike a kid on his first date, wondering whether she was going to let him kiss her at the end of it. Even though he knew she'd been raised like so many of the other women he'd been with, with privilege and security, he didn't sense in her the brittle sophistication, the eager search for new thrills that he'd seen so often in both sexes of her social class. It must be because her mother had sheltered her when she was younger. Lord knew Deidre had guarded her daughter as fiercely as a mother wolf since Ryan had known them.

He owed Jessica's mother a debt of gratitude for her support of him, he supposed, but he couldn't help but wonder about her agenda in all this. There was a hardness beneath Deidre's expensively-maintained exterior that he found disconcerting, and he didn't altogether trust her intentions.

"My favorite actor's a toss-up between Sean Connery and Mel Gibson," Jessica replied. "How about you?"

"I can't remember the last time I saw a movie," he found himself admitting, wishing he'd selected a subject he knew more about. Stock trading perhaps? He used to take his sisters to the Saturday matinees whenever he could collect enough bottles to raise the ticket money. Since he'd reached adulthood, he'd been too busy to waste time in a darkened theater when he could be cutting deals and adding to his fortune.

She leaned forward and laced her fingers together around her knee. "So what do you do when you aren't working?"

He knew what he'd like to be doing. His body remembered the way her soft curves had snugged up against him when they were sprawled in the snow. He'd probably left an imprint of his overheated body there. A smile quirked the corners of his mouth and his mind blanked like an empty computer screen.

She must have read something perverted into his smile, because her cheeks turned bright pink. "This won't work if you don't make an effort," she said primly.

"John Wayne," he blurted, grabbing at straws.

"John Wayne is your favorite actor?" she echoed. "He's been dead for years!"

"I warned you that it had been a while since I've been to the movies," he reminded her, gratified that he'd thought of someone besides one of the Disney characters he'd loved as a child.

Her nearness was damn distracting. As her hair dried into shimmering apricot waves, the edges caressing the line of her jaw, he was tempted to catch a silken strand between his fingers and to bury his nose in its depths. When he'd first seen her back in Willow Springs, her hair had brushed her shoulders.

"I like it shorter," he said, gesturing as he resisted the urge to tuck a wayward strand behind her ear. "When did you cut it?"

She bit her lip as she studied him silently, and he didn't think she was going to answer. The question wasn't that hard. Finally she sighed, drawing his attention to the movement of her chest.

"This length brings out the curl."

Ryan searched her upturned face. Unwittingly he'd just given her another opportunity to protest her identity, and yet she hadn't taken it. He debated asking what she was up to, and then he noticed the warmth in her gaze and the way her lips were softly parted.

In the space of a heartbeat, satisfying his curiosity about her abrupt change in tactics lost its importance. He lowered his head slowly, giving her plenty of opportunity to resist. When she didn't, he finally touched his lips to hers.

The shock of the kiss went through him like the

jolt from an exposed wire. It was at that moment, when he sank into the moist heat of her mouth and he heard her soft moan, that Ryan realized he had just made a huge tactical error of his own.

Chapter Six

Sarah stiffened when Ryan kissed her, but the warmth of his mouth, the gentleness of his touch melted the last shreds of her resistance like individual snowflakes landing on her outstretched hand. She meant only to blunt the sharp edges of her curiosity about him, but his low groan and the way his fingers bit into her shoulders ignited a response deep inside her that she could no more deny than her next breath.

Her fingers tangled in the heavy silk at his nape as she allowed him the entrance he sought, and she arched into him when his arms pinned her close. His mouth was hot on hers as he deepened the kiss. The blood pumping through her bubbled and flowed like a river of fire, her nerve endings sparking. His grip shifted, his fingers cupping her face before they plunged into her hair to hold her still for the ravishment of his tongue.

If she'd been standing, she was sure she would have fallen. As it was, she clung fiercely, desperately, her bones dissolving, her mind emptying, her mouth giving all he asked and more.

He shifted, urging her closer yet. Then the room spun behind her closed eyes and she felt the soft leather of the couch against her back as he laid her down. Winding her arms around his neck, she held on tight, willing the wild ride to go on and on until they burned each other up in a final explosion.

Sarah twisted restlessly, a whimper of unfamiliar hunger in her throat as he nibbled his way along her jaw to the rim of her ear, seeking out each sensitive nerve ending as he went. Her fingers plucked and clung and finally slipped beneath the tail of his shirt to stroke his bare skin, as smooth and warm as hand-rubbed wood. He shivered at her touch and she gloried in his response to her.

To *her,* Sarah Daniels. Call her what he would, it was her mouth, her touch and, as near as she could tell from the feel of his arousal, her body he wanted right now.

Too soon he levered himself away from her. Sarah's eyelids fluttered open reluctantly. Wasn't calling a halt the woman's job? She wished she had more experience, but Dan was always so controlled—so damn polite—and there hadn't been any really serious boyfriends before him.

When she looked up at Ryan, he was leaning against the back of the couch and staring up at the ceiling. If his chest hadn't been heaving as though he'd just run a marathon, she might wonder if she'd imagined the kiss—or dreamed it.

"What's wrong?" Her voice sounded timid to her ears. Did he regret what had just taken place between them? It certainly changed things, but perhaps he hadn't been as affected as she after all, and now he was regretting having abducted her in the first place.

A bubble of hysterical laughter rose in her throat. Wouldn't that be a fine mess, as her father used to say?

"Nothing's wrong." Ryan's voice was flat, but he clasped her hand in his. Lifting it to his mouth, he turned so he was looking at her more fully as he brushed his lips across her knuckles. "I didn't expect that."

"Didn't expect to kiss me?" she asked, puzzled. "Do you always map out every move ahead of time?"

"Obviously not, or you wouldn't be here."

Was it regret she heard in his voice? How had she ever thought little nobody Sarah Daniels could hold the attention of a man like him, even while he thought she was someone else? Dan had been the only man to see past her shyness and take an interest, but she'd certainly messed that up.

Ryan dropped her hand and got to his feet, pacing in front of the fire as Quincy's gaze followed him. Ryan stopped and scrubbed one hand over his face.

Even with whiskers shadowing his jaw, he managed to look like just what he was, a successful, sophisticated male in his prime. Helpless to squelch her reaction, Sarah wished he would kiss her again.

"This is getting complicated," he said.

Before she could ask what he meant, a tinny-sounding ring interrupted them. It came from his briefcase on the floor by the couch.

"Dammit," Ryan exclaimed, "I'd better get that. It's got to be your grandfather making sure I'm not compromising you."

Sarah didn't know how to take his comment. And what if this man wanted to talk to *her?* Would he be able to tell from her voice that she wasn't Jessica? He'd thought her newspaper photo was his granddaughter. Was the man getting senile?

Watching Ryan dial the combination and unlock his case, Sarah realized that she was no longer sure she wanted to get away from him. Not until she had a chance to explore further the way his kisses made her feel.

She held her breath while he answered the call, but the signal must have been too weak. It was obvious he couldn't understand the voice on the other end. After several shouted attempts to make contact, he finally gave up.

"If you can hear what I'm saying, we're both fine." He glanced at Sarah. Her heart stuttered, but he didn't hold out the phone. "I'll call you back later," he said instead before he switched it off and put it away with a look of disgust.

"Useless waste of technology," he muttered.

Not quite ready to face him, Sarah allowed her gaze to wander around the room as she rubbed her forearms, chilled despite the fire on the hearth. What on earth was she considering? Had she lost her mind?

"It's so quiet here," she said, getting to her feet restlessly. "Don't you have a radio or anything? What kind of music do you like?"

"Music?" Ryan frowned as though the concept was a foreign one. "I guess I don't usually listen to anything."

"Not even when you're in the car?" she asked. "How can you stand the silence?" Funny, it didn't usually bother her, but now the quiet ground against her nerve endings like the strident sounds of heavy metal.

"When I'm driving I play motivational tapes or I tune in the news," he replied. "I guess after growing up with two sisters, I've learned to appreciate the lack of noise. How about you?"

She barely remembered the first five years of her life, bounced around from one foster home to another before she'd been adopted by the older, childless couple. "I wanted siblings and laughter, not the silence of being an only child."

"I understand you play the piano very well," he said. "I'm sorry I don't have one, but we could correct that."

Her eyes widened. "Yes, how did you know?" Ever since she'd seen a woman playing in a store window shortly after her arrival in Bellville, Sarah had bugged her adoptive parents for lessons until they finally relented. For the first couple of years she'd daydreamed about a concert career, of becoming so famous that her birth parents would see her and regret giving her up. Now she played for her own pleasure.

Ryan frowned at her question. "Your mother told me about the piano. She said you took to it from the beginning and never had to be reminded to practice, unlike ballet, which you detested."

What a coincidence that Jessica loved music, too. Sarah was fairly certain she would have detested ballet lessons. She wanted to ask if he was certain his intended hadn't been adopted, but since Sarah had remained in the system until she was five, surely someone would have known if a twin existed.

"You never took music lessons?" she asked Ryan. "Not the drums, or even the kazoo?"

His grin was fleeting. "Our budget didn't stretch that far. At one point I wanted desperately to play in the school band so I could impress a certain girl, but you had to lease an instrument and it was out of the question." He shrugged. "The girl moved away and I switched my allegiance to sports."

Sarah brightened and then she realized she couldn't say anything about her softball. What had he told her Jessica played? Tennis and golf. Sarah didn't know enough about either to discuss it intelligently. "Which sports were you in?" she asked him.

"Sandlot baseball and pickup basketball in the school yard whenever I could get out of watching my sisters."

"Didn't you play on any organized teams?" Sarah could picture him in a uniform, surrounded by cheerleaders and impressionable groupies.

He shook his head. "I always worked after school."

"Oh." She wasn't sure what to say. Her parents hadn't been rich, but they'd provided the necessities and had money for some extras. "Doing what?"

"Anything that paid money, from collecting bottles to a paper route, mowing lawns, flipping burgers." He looked down at his hands. "You name it, I've done it."

"I used to baby-sit," Sarah blurted, and then she realized from the change in his expression as he surged to his feet that she'd said the wrong thing.

"For what?" he sneered. "Pocket change? You don't need to patronize me." His voice was harsh as he reached for her. "We may come from different backgrounds, but there's one thing we've found in common, haven't we?"

He took advantage of Sarah's shock to cover her mouth with his in a bold kiss that swept past her defenses and plunged her into a vortex of feeling. Overwhelmed by the sensual onslaught, she could only hold on as she responded wholeheartedly to his passion. As abruptly as it began, the kiss was over and he set her firmly away from him. Her legs barely held her up, her knees as weak as under-brewed coffee.

Self-disgust washed over Ryan when he saw her dazed expression and the flush on her normally creamy cheeks. Her eyes had darkened, her lips swollen from his assault. Acting like an animal wasn't going to further his cause, nor was it going to make their stay here together any more pleasant—for either of them.

He'd assumed Jessica had plenty of experience. It was hardly the kind of thing he could have asked her mother about, but her response to him made him realize she hadn't been around as much as he'd figured. With a parent like Deidre watching over her, it shouldn't have been a surprise.

The situation wasn't helped by his suspicion that seducing Jessica while they were alone here wouldn't be very difficult, not the way she melted against him when he touched her. If only Stuart didn't trust him so much!

Too bad she cast a spell that threatened to completely undermine Ryan's good intentions. Sweet-talking her into bed had seemed too calculated, even for him, so he'd opted for the reasonable approach instead. Now he was the one in danger of being seduced. What a tangled web, as his mother used to say.

"W-why are you looking at me like that?" Jessica asked, her arms folded protectively across those alluring curves. He could still remember just how they'd felt pressed against him. How he'd like to mold them with his hands, feel her nipples tighten in response to his touch. Seeing her wearing his clothes shouldn't have been erotic, but it was.

"You're very alluring," he said without thinking.

To his surprise, her eyes widened and then she turned away with a frown of annoyance. "You don't have to say that."

She must get hit on all the time, even with Deidre hovering around, but she acted like his comment made her uncomfortable—not as if she expected something more flowery and poetic, but as though she didn't realize how pretty she was. How could that be? Did she think men only pursued her because of her family's fortune?

Wasn't that exactly what Ryan was doing?

"I don't say things I don't mean." He kept his voice low as he watched her carefully. Maybe she needed to be wooed, not because he was a manipulative bastard, but because she had no real clue that even if she were penniless, men would want her. He'd gone about this all wrong; he could see that now.

The mistake had cost him precious time, but the heavy snowfall outside might just remedy that. Unless it stopped soon, they weren't going anywhere for a while.

She looked at him and shrugged. "Okay, sure."

Ryan approached her carefully. "You can't be so naive that you think I can fake my reaction to you."

The color in her cheeks deepened. Interesting oxymoron, an heiress who could still blush. "Isn't that kind of automatic?" she stammered, keeping her gaze on his face.

"Only until a guy reaches his twenties. After that a little discrimination kicks in, at least for some of us." When she turned her head away, he ran his hand down her arm, feeling the tremors, and captured her wrist. "Let's give this a try," he suggested. "You're not indifferent to me—"

Her gaze flew to his.

"I'm not wrong, am I?" he persisted gently, lifting her hand and pressing his mouth to the inside of her wrist where her pulse scrambled and raced.

Her only response was to shake her head, making her hair swirl like the fringe on a dancer's costume.

"There's your grandfather and the business to consider," he added. "And it's what your mother wants, too." How could she refuse when there were so many compelling reasons to agree?

She stiffened and he realized he'd said too much. Even a greenhorn knew the danger of overselling.

"What about love?" Her voice was little more than a whisper.

"What about it?" His hand tightened on hers. Not *that* again. Why did women always bring it up at the most inconvenient times? *Tell me you love me, even if all we both want is to jump into bed.* Did Jessica expect the words, too, even if they were hollow? He wanted her, but love? That was a place he wasn't about to go, not even to pull off the deal of the century. The idea of giving up that much control to someone else was too damn scary.

He'd had relationships; mutual respect, hot sex and a friendly goodbye at the end were all he needed. It had only been when a woman claimed to love him and didn't want to let go, even after he'd walked in on her with a friend of his, that things had gotten messy. The experience had reinforced Ryan's determination to avoid Cupid's arrow at all costs.

Jessica's gaze darted away from his. "You deserve to be loved for yourself," she said, surprising him. "It makes me sad that you'd consider marriage without it, even to an heiress."

This was getting too damn deep for him. "Don't do me any favors," he said sharply. "You want a beer? Some wine?"

"A glass of wine would be nice," she replied, lacing her fingers together. "Do you think the snow will stop soon?"

"We're stuck here until it does," he tossed over his shoulder on the way to the kitchen.

Sarah watched him go, his words sinking in. Not too long ago, she'd been dying to get out of here, and now she was grateful for the possibility they'd be spending even more time here. For what? So he could fall in love with her? She whirled as though she could dodge the thought. Besides, hadn't he made his feelings crystal-clear on that subject?

She thought about the woman he intended to wed. What were the chances that a pampered princess who'd been groomed to make an advantageous marriage and smart business deal could bring happiness to a complicated man like Ryan? The more time Sarah spent with him, the more obvious it became that he needed a woman capable of seeing through his arrogant exterior to the lonely man who denied his own emotions because he was afraid of being abandoned.

He came back with two goblets and handed one to Sarah. "What are you plotting now?" he asked.

Her only reply was a secretive smile that made him nervous. Not that he cared what she was up to if it warmed her toward him and the deal he offered.

He clinked his wineglass against hers. "Here's to our future," he said, testing her.

She raised her glass in acknowledgment and sipped from it, her gaze meeting his over the rim. At least she hadn't run screaming from the room. So why did that make him wary rather than pleased?

He was about to take a drink of his own wine when Quincy went to the door and whimpered. When Ryan looked out the window, the snow was still coming down heavily. He let Quincy out, watching as the dog waded through the deep drifts to his favorite spot. When he was done, Ryan waited expectantly for him to come back inside. Instead the dog's ears perked up and he quivered all over as he stared intently in the direction of the Jeep.

"Uh-oh," Ryan muttered as he spotted the rabbit that had claimed Quincy's attention. "Come on, boy!"

The dog ignored his sharp command.

Jessica joined him at the door. "What's wrong?"

Just as he pointed, the rabbit took off through the snow in great leaps with Quincy in hot pursuit.

"Oh, no!" Jessica exclaimed. "The poor bunny."

"Quincy will never catch it." Ryan called his name a couple more times, but the dog didn't even slow down.

"What should we do?" Jessica asked, gripping Ryan's arm. "He'll freeze out there."

"No, it's not that cold. He'll lose interest and come back." When the dog disappeared through the trees, Ryan shut the door. "Let's watch for him through the window."

To his surprise, Jessica didn't let go of his arm as the minutes went by and they both waited for a flash of red to appear against the stark black and white landscape of snow and trees. He could feel the side of her breast pressing against him.

"He must have gotten lost," she said finally.

Despite the distraction of her nearness, Ryan was getting concerned as well. He hoped the silly mutt hadn't strayed too far. "He'll be able to follow his own trail right back here."

"Unless he's hurt."

"He was chasing a rabbit, not a bear," he pointed out as his unease increased. The dog should have run out of steam and returned by now. It wouldn't take long for his tracks to disappear.

"Maybe we should go look for him."

Ryan was about to disagree when he looked down and saw the way her eyes glistened. "Oh, God, don't cry," he groaned, unable to resist the watery plea. "I'll find him."

He glanced longingly at the cozy fire and their wineglasses sitting side by side on the end table. Slogging through the snow after an animal that didn't have the sense to know its own limitations wasn't how he'd planned to spend the next couple of hours, but a brisk walk in the crisp air might whip his libido back into submission. He was growing way too aware of Jessica's considerable physical assets.

"I'm going with you," she replied.

"It would be too difficult for you to walk in deep snow in those oversized boots," he argued, needing the break from her company.

She angled her chin. "You're not leaving me behind to stand at the window and wring my hands."

What if they couldn't find Quincy, or something bad had happened to him? Ryan would rather spare her, in case the dog had run into a bear or a cougar. "You'd just slow me down."

"No, I won't." It was clear from her stubborn expression that he would only lose valuable time by arguing further.

"All right."

"Thank you," Jessica murmured, ignoring his ungracious tone as she reached up to kiss his cheek.

For a moment, Ryan was tempted to pull her into his arms, but he resisted. Instead he unlocked the closet where he'd tossed their outerwear earlier. "Dress warm while I collect a few things." He pulled on his boots and his old down parka. "I'll be right back for you."

After he'd donned a stocking cap and gloves, he stuffed a lightweight blanket from the shelf into a backpack, just in case. Then he headed outside to the shed as he composed a mental list of what he needed.

When he came in with the full pack and a coiled rope on one shoulder, Jessica frowned. "You do think he's gotten into some kind of trouble," she said accusingly.

"Naw, I just like to be prepared for anything." They had to be idiots, going out in a storm to look for a dog they hadn't known existed until yesterday.

He tossed her another stocking cap. "Here, wear this." While she complied, he ducked into the kitchen, but he didn't mention that he was taking the first aid kit as well as a hatchet, a knife and a lantern, in case they didn't find Quincy before dark or they got lost. If there had been a rifle at the cabin, he would have taken it, too, but he wasn't into hunting and keeping guns around made him nervous.

Once they got outside, Sarah was relieved to see that Quincy's trail, crisscrossing the rabbit's tracks, was still visible. As Ryan led the way to break a path for her, she marveled at how safe she felt in his company despite the swirling white all around them. Certainly she didn't always agree with him, but she was beginning to trust his judgment—at least in some areas.

Before they were out of sight of the cabin, he took a spray can from his pocket and shook it hard, rattling the metal ball inside.

"What's that for?" Sarah asked.

"It's orange spray paint I found in the cupboard. I figured I'd mark the tree trunks in case our tracks get covered up." To illustrate, he sprayed a streak at eye level on a nearby fir.

"It certainly beats leaving a trail of bread crumbs,"

Sarah commented, realizing for the first time how easy it would be to get lost out here.

The crisp air she drew into her lungs as they walked reminded her of the smells of Christmases with the Daniels; the freshly cut tree they decorated together, the hot cider they gave out to the carolers who came by, the holiday dinner they always shared with a motley mix of friends and acquaintances who had no families in the area.

How different Jessica Walker's holidays must have been, filled with glittering parties, elegant clothes, fancy refreshments and piles of expensive gifts. And what of Ryan's childhood memories? Sarah would have liked to ask more about his family, but she had to save her breath. The silence around them was nearly reverential. Even the tromping of their feet was muffled.

Every a few minutes Ryan stopped to whistle sharply or to shake the paint can hard and spray another tree. Sarah listened hard for Quincy's bark, but she heard nothing. Her stomach tightened. She'd really expected to see a tired, wet dog come trotting toward them through the woods before now, tongue lolling.

"He's probably got that rabbit cornered in a burrow and he's too busy to hear us," Ryan said over his shoulder as he moved ahead.

"Probably," she echoed, willing to bet he didn't believe what he was saying any more than she did. The tightness in her stomach was gathering into a huge knot. What if Ryan decided they had to turn back before they were able to find the Irish Setter to whom she'd already grown quite attached? Could the poor animal survive another night outdoors?

Sarah walked with her head down, blinking back tears that blurred her vision and made her stumble. She was wiping her nose on a bandanna handkerchief she'd found folded in the pocket of her borrowed parka when Ryan stopped again.

"How are you doing?" he asked, his expelled breath forming a cloud as his gaze swept over her. "Warm enough?"

Sarah wasn't about to admit how cold her cheeks were or how tiring walking had become in the clumsy boots. He'd insist she return to the cabin, would probably waste valuable time accompanying her when they could be continuing their search.

"I'm fine." She turned to look back, dismayed by the way their tracks disappeared only yards behind them. At least the orange paint was still visible against the nearly black tree bark. She glanced upward, but the descending snowflakes made her dizzy. "How long until dark?"

Ryan squinted at the sky. "Less than an hour, I'd imagine, but we don't dare stay out here that long. The snow's falling too hard to risk it."

She gestured impatiently. "Shouldn't we keep going?"

His mouth tightened. "Yes, of course." Skirting a stand of yellow pine, he trudged on. Every few moments he paused to use the paint and to call out, hands cupped around his mouth.

No joyful bark greeted them, not even a whine. The jagged line of disturbed snow was becoming more difficult to follow, but Ryan kept going. Whenever they crossed a bare patch beneath the trees, he would drop back to walk with Sarah on the carpet of fir needles.

"Something must have happened to him," she said, struggling against a growing sense of discouragement. "We're running out of time, aren't we?" Even as she spoke, the light was fading and they still had to find their own way back to the cabin.

"We're not quitting just yet." Ryan's determination gave her hope. He stopped to enfold her in a reassuring hug. She clung to him, his cold cheek resting against hers, until he lowered his arms again and stepped back. Then he dug into his pocket and brought out a granola bar. Breaking it in two, he gave half to Sarah. While she munched on her share, forcing herself to ignore her growing sense of urgency and take a much-needed break, she watched him through her lashes. His white teeth bit into his piece of the snack bar, the muscles of his jaw flexing as he chewed. When he swallowed, his throat worked in a way she found fascinating.

She didn't realize she was staring until he arched his brows in silent query. There was a knowing expression in his light eyes, such a contrast to his tanned cheeks and the red of his stocking cap.

Blinking, she finished her portion and brushed her gloves together. "Did you ever have a dog?" she asked, wanting to distract him from his awareness that she'd been staring like a teenager with a crush.

"We had a cocker mix named Queenie for a while," he replied. "What about you?"

"We usually had a cat or two." She searched the landscape for any sign of Quincy, but visibility was limited to a few yards in any direction.

"I'm surprised Deidre allowed them on the premises."

She didn't know how to answer that. "What happened to your dog?" she asked instead.

He shrugged as he tucked the granola bar wrapper into his pocket and shifted the coiled rope from one arm to the other. "She led a happy life and finally died in her sleep."

"Do you have any pets now?" she persisted as they set out again. She had no idea whether he had a house or a condo, or where it was located. Now, however, she was reluctant to reveal her ignorance of things Jessica would probably know about him.

"I've got two tanks of saltwater fish," he replied. "Not very cuddly, but watching them relaxes me."

"Do you have trouble relaxing?" she asked, floundering in an uneven spot and nearly falling before she managed to right herself.

When she'd regained her footing, she realized that Ryan had stopped again under a stand of trees to mark another trunk with paint. He didn't immediately move on.

"What's wrong?" she asked as he looked one way and then another.

When he glanced at Sarah, his expression was grim. "I'm not sure which direction to take. I've lost his tracks."

It was true. The way the Douglas firs were grouped made it impossible to tell which way Quincy might have gone around them. Both Sarah and Ryan circled the trees with heads bowed, looking for a sign that hadn't been obliterated by the falling snow.

"Perhaps if we fanned out—" she suggested.

"No. We stay together. I'm not losing you, too."

He'd already given up. Fresh tears welled in her eyes at the thought of abandoning Quincy to the elements. "And I'm not going back without him," she declared rashly. Part of her knew she was being unreasonable, but she didn't care.

To her relief, Ryan gave a jerky nod. "We'll give it a few more minutes." He glanced around and then he pointed. "Let's try—" He stopped abruptly, head cocked.

"What?" Sarah asked, when he didn't move.

Instead of replying, he raised one hand for silence. "What was that noise?" he asked after a moment in which she was afraid to breathe.

At first she didn't hear anything. Ears straining, she stared at Ryan, praying he'd been right as he turned in a wide circle, his whistle piercing the translucent curtain of snow that surrounded them. This time the response was faint but recognizable, a whine that sent her heart climbing into her throat. Head snapping around, Ryan let out a shout of triumph and then he broke into an awkward trot through the snow.

''Come on!'' he exclaimed without looking back. ''That damn dog's still alive!''

Tears of relief obscuring her vision, Sarah struggled along after him. In moments they were standing at the edge of a steep gully. Below them on a narrow ledge where he had obviously fallen lay Quincy. He was motionless, the fiery red of his coat already partially obscured by a thin blanket of snow.

Chapter Seven

Ryan stared down at the dog with mingled relief and dismay. He was aware that Jessica had come up beside him, her gloved hand clamped to her mouth as she gazed over the edge of the steep drop.

At first Ryan had figured his main reason for coming after Quincy in the snowstorm was to please her, but while they searched, he'd realized how badly he wanted the dog to be all right.

The animal's uncomplicated affection reminded Ryan of the little cocker mix he hadn't thought about in years. Since he'd discovered Queenie that last morning, he'd never even considered replacing her. It hadn't seemed worth the pain of inevitable loss. Now he wasn't so sure. All he knew at the moment was that Quincy deserved better than to die in the snow and the cold.

"We heard him," Jessica said softly. "He's got to be okay."

"He's probably just worn-out," Ryan replied, hoping he was right. The dog's chest was moving, so at least he was breathing. Ryan didn't allow himself to wonder what they'd do if the dog was badly injured. First they had to get him off that ledge before they lost what little daylight was left. At least the snow seemed to be slowing a little.

"What are you doing?" he asked when Jessica walked along the edge of the drop.

"I'm looking for a way down," she replied.

"You aren't going anywhere. I'll get him." Uncoiling the rope, Ryan tied one end to a nearby tree and tugged on it experimentally. The pine felt sturdy enough to hold him. He slipped off the backpack and looped the other end of the rope beneath his arms.

"But I'm a lot lighter than you are," Jessica argued, eyeing the tree dubiously. "And I'm perfectly capable of climbing down there."

Ryan suppressed his impatience and grasped her by the shoulders. "I don't doubt that for a minute," he said, knowing there was no way he would allow her to take that kind of risk. "But how are you going to get Quincy back up here?"

She bit her lip, her eyes huge in her pale face. "How are you?"

He pulled the blanket from the backpack. "I've done some climbing. There are plenty of handholds and we're lucky he's only a little too far down to jump up on his own. I might be able to boost him up. If not, I'll rig a sling with this. You can toss it down to me if I need it.''

He didn't bother to comment on what they'd do if Quincy was badly hurt. Leaving him there in the growing darkness wasn't an option.

The sounds of their voices must have attracted the dog's attention, because he opened his eyes and barked sharply, bringing a smile of relief to Jessica's face, and then he rolled from his side to his stomach, nearly toppling from the edge of the shelf as he attempted to stand up.

Jessica's smile turned to a gasp of fright. Some doggy radar must have communicated his precarious position, because he stopped moving and looked up at them with beseeching eyes.

Grabbing Jessica's face between his hands, Ryan gave her a quick, hard kiss on her cold lips. ''Talk to him,'' he told her. ''Keep him calm.''

She gulped and nodded.

''I'll get him,'' Ryan promised rashly. ''Here, feed out the slack on the rope as I need it, so it doesn't get in my way.''

Luckily Quincy seemed to understand the danger, because except for crawling closer to the rock face on his belly, the only thing he moved was his tail. It thumped twice, dislodging the snow clinging to it, and then it, too, went still as if he was waiting to be rescued.

"Be careful," Jessica told Ryan as he tugged on the rope one last time, testing it.

He gave her a wink and then he eased himself over the edge, groping for hand and footholds. He could hear Jessica's voice as she did what he had asked, crooning softly to the dog and telling him what a good boy he was.

With reluctance, Ryan blocked out the sound of her voice and concentrated on the task at hand. It had been a long time since he'd done any serious climbing, but he hadn't forgotten the basic skills.

The first few feet were sloped rather than being sheer, and then it only took a couple more moments to reach the dog. Once his boots were planted firmly on the outcropping of rock, Ryan removed his gloves and patted Quincy's head. Ryan didn't see any blood on the dog's fur, but it was getting difficult to see in the fading light, so he ran his hands over Quincy's ribs and legs, talking to him all the while and testing for tenderness. Miraculously, except for a couple of scrapes, Quincy seemed okay.

Ryan looked up to where he could just make out Jessica's head peering over the edge. "He's in good shape," he called out to her.

Her thumbs-up gesture made Ryan feel like a hero.

"How are you going to bring him up?" she asked. "Do you want the blanket for a sling?"

The wall above the ledge extended vertically for about five feet up before it sloped at an angle. There had been no way Quincy could have managed on his own but, with luck, if Ryan lifted him he could scramble the rest of the way to the top. As long as the dog didn't struggle too much and knock Ryan off the ledge.

Quickly he told Jessica what he intended to do. "If you lie on your stomach, you should be able to grab him and help to pull him up," he concluded.

Her head bobbed. "Be careful, both of you."

If Ryan lost his balance when he lifted Quincy, he'd get banged up, but the rope would probably keep him from falling all the way to the bottom of the gully. Ryan didn't want to think what would happen to Quincy if he dropped the dog. They were running out of time and this was their best shot. Giving the dog a last reassuring stroke, Ryan picked him up.

Sarah watched with her heart firmly wedged in her throat as Ryan scooped the Irish Setter into his arms and straightened with agonizing slowness. Suddenly the ledge appeared way too narrow, the jumble of boulders below too unforgiving despite their deceptive cloak of snow. She had to bite down hard on her lip to keep a useless warning from popping out to distract him.

For a moment, Ryan swayed and she forgot to breathe. Then he regained his balance. The expression on his usually hard face as he spoke to the dog was astonishingly tender. The image of Quincy nestled so trustingly in his arms was one Sarah wouldn't soon forget.

A wave of emotion surged through her. There was so much more to Ryan than she had first realized. He had a good heart.

Her breath caught as he lifted the dog even higher. Miraculously, Quincy didn't struggle.

While Sarah waited, afraid to move, Ryan inched the setter up to the break in the wall where the ground began to slope. As if he understood perfectly what Ryan was trying to do, Quincy planted his front feet on the slight incline. With a last boost from behind, he scrambled high enough for Sarah to grasp his fur and help him over the top. She gave him a quick hug while he washed her cheek with his tongue, and then she turned back to Ryan.

To her amazement, he was already halfway back up to the top. She pulled up the slack in the rope as his head appeared. The moment he crawled over the edge and collapsed beside her, Sarah wrapped her arms around him and burst into tears.

Ryan's whole body went still as he held her close. The snow, he realized distractedly, had finally stopped falling. His glance darted to the dog who, looking no worse for wear, stood watching them both with his head cocked to the side, his tail wagging slowly.

"What's the matter?" Ryan asked the woman sobbing into his parka. He was completely confused by her outburst. She'd held up so well, only to fall apart now that the rescue operation was all but complete.

Ryan patted her clumsily on her back. He could feel her trembling. "I told you, Quincy seems fine. If the ledge had been any closer, he probably could have managed without our help."

"It's not Quincy I'm concerned about right now," she gulped against his shoulder. "It's you."

With a frown of annoyance, Deidre Walker glanced down at the manicure she'd managed to ruin by picking at the bloodred polish. Why hadn't Ryan called back?

Stuart had been worried about the mountain storm ever since he'd heard the weather report and she'd finally had all she could take of his endless fussing. Now she stood at the window of her spacious private sitting room on the second floor and stared out at the formal gardens without really noticing them.

She had a lot more to worry about than a little snow! What if Ryan failed to persuade Jessica to marry him? Granted, as a teenager she'd become a little more difficult for Deidre to manage, but she'd always fallen into line sooner or later. Didn't it just figure that now, when the stakes were higher than they'd ever been, Jessica would choose to defy her!

Deidre's plan to play matchmaker and pair Jessica with her grandfather's protégé, thus ensuring her own position in one of the region's wealthiest families, had been a brilliant one. Ryan was not only rich in his own right, but he was as handsome as sin and he'd been surprisingly receptive to the idea of marrying Jessica and keeping his mentor happy. The only problem had been that once Deidre outlined the plan to her daughter, the silly girl had bolted without giving Ryan a chance.

Didn't she understand that if she annoyed Stuart

sufficiently, he could very well cut both her and her mother off without a penny? Lord knew he'd been indifferent enough to his only grandchild for years after her father was killed. It was only recently, as Stuart's own mortality stared him in the face, that he'd made an effort to become more involved in her future.

Choosing her husband might seem a trifle Victorian to some people, but it had given Deidre yet another opportunity to fulfill Stuart's wishes and stay on his good side. The only reason she was still here was that she'd been shrewd enough to present him with Lawrence's child. If not for Jessica, Deidre had no doubt she would have been tossed out on her shapely behind years ago.

Besides, Ryan Noble would make an excellent mate for her headstrong daughter. He was much too busy wheeling and dealing to impose himself on Jessica once they were wed and the novelty had worn off. She would have plenty of time to devote to the tiresome causes that had captured her interest for no reason Deidre could fathom. Here was a girl who could have enjoyed a lifestyle anyone would envy: membership in the best clubs, inclusion in the right circles, a constant stream of the most coveted invitations, but instead she chose to spend her time with people who were without exception her social inferiors.

Deidre turned away from the window to examine her reflection in the antique wall mirror. She needed to have her nails repaired in the morning. Perhaps she'd have André do something with her hair while she was at the salon. The sophisticated blond bob looked a little dull in the unforgiving daylight and she had a luncheon date with two of the worst gossips from her club.

Leaning closer to the mirror, she examined a tiny line between her brows that hadn't been there yesterday. She'd better schedule an appointment with her plastic surgeon. The strain of this whole situation with Jessica was starting to show.

Deliberately Deidre smoothed out her expression and took a deep, relaxing breath. Once she heard from Ryan that his courtship was progressing on schedule, she would be able to set her concerns at rest before they did permanent damage to her complexion.

Sarah lifted her face from where she'd buried it against Ryan's shoulder and tried to assess his reaction to her outburst. In her mind's eye she could still picture him on that narrow ledge, lifting Quincy. Ryan's balance had appeared to waver for one heart-stopping instant before he steadied himself and boosted the dog to safety. It must have been at that precise moment that Ryan had stolen her heart.

Not that she'd admit it—not to him, and only reluctantly to herself. What the heck had she let herself in for now? Ryan wasn't like Dan, who'd happily lived his whole life in Bellville with every intention of dying there. She was headed for heartache with no brakes.

"Did you mean what you said?" Ryan demanded

in a low, intense voice. "About being worried about me?"

Sarah levered herself away from him, shaken by what she'd just realized. "Actually the word I used was 'concerned'," she said in an attempt at lightness.

The glow in his eyes dimmed, making her feel like a wretch. He'd risked his life for Quincy, and she was brushing his heroism aside as though it didn't matter, just because her own raw feelings scared her.

"Yes," she admitted softly. "When I saw you on that ledge, I was terrified."

He blinked as though he hadn't expected her to be so blunt. Then he grinned as he pulled her to her feet. "Don't you think I deserve some kind of reward?" he asked outrageously.

For a moment Sarah chewed her lip as she pretended to ponder his suggestion, when it was all she could do to keep from covering his face with kisses— not unlike the dog he'd just rescued, she thought with a spurt of wry humor.

Ryan was so close she could see the individual whiskers along his jaw. "What did you have in mind?" she murmured.

His gaze flicked to her mouth, scorching her with its intensity. "I'll leave that up to you." His voice was husky, but his arms stayed at his sides. Clearly the next move was hers.

It was an easy one to make. Sliding her gloved hands up the front of his jacket, she gripped the sides of his collar in chilled fingers. "Come here," she whispered, giving in to the craving she could no longer ignore.

His lips were cool and firm, but they heated quickly on hers. She could sense the passion surging through him, but he allowed her control of the kiss, his mouth warm and pliant as she leaned into him and parted her lips. A tremor went through him at the first touch of her tongue, but still he held back.

Timidly at first, she explored his mouth, growing bolder as a raw groan rumbled up from his throat. Daringly she took the kiss deeper, testing his control. For a long moment he stood as rigid as a statue while she played the siren, exploring the extent of her new powers and the sensations they evoked.

Finally his control snapped and he grabbed her arms with steely fingers. Sarah pressed closer, sinking into his heat and his strength, glorying in the barely leashed energy that radiated from him as his mouth ravaged hers. Passion swirled through her as she clung to the only solid thing in a suddenly spinning world and then, too soon, it was over. His grip loosened as he lifted his head and broke the sensuous connection.

He stepped back, his chest expanding on a long, shaky breath. The icy gray of his eyes had turned to smoke. "Damn, your timing is something else. We'd better get going."

Unable to speak, Sarah brushed the snow from her clothes while he removed the loop of rope from around his torso. Had the embrace affected him as it did her? She felt as though her world was altered in ways she had yet to realize, and here he was making practical decisions.

She'd nearly forgotten all about poor Quincy. Her hands were still shaking with reaction when she picked up the blanket and began rubbing his coat with it.

"Is he really okay?" she asked, her voice unnaturally high. "Should we wrap him up?"

When she sneaked a peek at Ryan, he was watching her with an unreadable expression. She blamed the dusky color splashed across his cheekbones on the chill in the air.

"We'd better keep him warm," he said. "I'll carry him and you take the light. Now that the snow has stopped, the temperature will probably drop."

Opening the backpack, he switched on the lantern and handed it to her. Then he shrugged into the pack and took the blanket while she put the coiled rope over her shoulder.

Before she could move away, Ryan caught her sleeve. His eyes were narrowed, the message in their depths screened by his lashes. "When we get back to the cabin, we'll talk. You can bet on it."

Sarah opened her mouth, but no words came out. He proceeded to wrap Quincy up like a baby in the blanket. Hefting the swaddled dog into his arms, he signaled for Sarah to move out. With the beam from the lantern to guide them, they began the trek back to the cabin.

The only sounds were Ryan's low voice as he reassured Quincy, the crunch of their footsteps and the

sigh of the wind as it blew through the treetops overhead. Sarah was tired, cold and elated they'd found
the dog in relatively good health, but her overriding
emotion during the walk back to the cabin was ap-
prehension.

Sooner or later, Ryan was going to find out she
wasn't Jessica. The odds that he might prefer ordinary
Sarah Daniels over a sophisticated heiress might be
pretty long, the game being one she hadn't asked to
play, but now that she was in, she was powerless to
resist gambling everything she had on the outcome.

"We made it!" Jessica exclaimed with a glance
over her shoulder at Ryan.

No one could have been happier to see the cabin's
peaked roof in the lantern beam than he was. He was
glad Jessica hadn't seemed to realize the risks in
tramping unarmed through the wilderness in the dark.
At the very least, they could have lost their way. The
tracks they'd made heading out had disappeared under a coat of new snow almost a mile back. They'd
missed one of the marks he'd blazed on a tree trunk
and had nearly wandered off course. Getting lost
wasn't the only danger. Although the only creature
they'd encountered was an owl, cougars and bears
weren't unheard of in the area.

He'd had no business allowing her to go with him.
If anything had happened to her, the blame would
have been entirely his.

Now that the journey was over, he was aware that
his arms ached from carrying the dog, his sore shoul-

der throbbed and his cheek was numb from being licked. Whenever Quincy had grown restless and started to struggle in Ryan's arms, he'd done his best to soothe the dog with the sound of his voice. Each time Ryan spoke, Quincy swiped whatever part of Ryan's face that his tongue could reach. With Ryan's arms otherwise occupied, he'd had no defense against the affectionate onslaught.

At least Quincy's antics had distracted him from staring holes through the back of Jessica's stocking cap while he wondered what was going on in her head. Saying she'd begun to thaw toward him was like calling the obstacle that had taken out the Titanic an ice cube. The kiss she'd given him had nearly singed his socks despite the cold air surrounding them. He'd tried to convince himself she was just overreacting to Quincy's rescue, but Ryan hoped with every aroused cell of his being that the dog had no part of what had taken place between Jessica and himself.

"Would you like a cup of cocoa?" she asked once he'd set Quincy down to answer nature's call and then they'd all trouped into the cabin. Amazingly, the dog didn't even limp. "I saw a couple of packets and a bag of marshmallows in the cupboard earlier."

Ryan would have preferred something stronger to thaw him from the inside out, but he needed to keep a clear head. She'd already laid a serious threat on his control, and the last thing he wanted was to misread the signals she was giving and push her farther than she was ready to go.

He realized now that seducing her wasn't enough. He wanted more than for her to be swept along by his desire; he wanted Jessica to need him as badly as he did her. If their last kiss was any indication, the new goal he'd set for himself was an obtainable one.

"Cocoa sounds good," he said as he helped her out of her jacket and hung it over a chair to dry out. She'd pulled off her cap and was finger-combing the damp hair flattened to her head. Ryan ignored the lure of her full lips as he unzipped his parka.

"Why don't you feed Quincy and I'll get the fire built up," he suggested. "Good thing the caretaker left us a case of hash."

Her eyebrows rose. "You have a caretaker? That's why the cabin was stocked with food?"

"Yeah, he's an old vet on a pension who lives in a trailer a few miles down the road. I met him in the woods one day picking mushrooms."

Her look of dawning comprehension suddenly made frustrating sense to him. "You didn't believe me when I told you I never planned this."

Her gaze shifted away from his. "I wasn't sure."

He caught her chin with his fingers, lifting her head so she had to look at him. "I may be far from perfect, but I don't lie. That's something you'll figure out about me in time, I guess."

She pulled away from his light grip. "Neither do I," she said quietly.

"Then why did you insist you're not Jessica?" he demanded.

The flush on her cheeks deepened. "I was scared,"

she mumbled, "and that's the truth. Now, if you don't mind, I'd better feed Quincy. He's probably famished."

Ryan watched her walk away, frustration bunching his hands into fists at his sides. Quincy circled her with as much energy as if he'd spent the afternoon in front of the fire instead of being trapped on a ledge in the cold. At least the darned dog wasn't any worse for the ordeal.

The jury was still out on his human rescuers.

Ryan had to remind himself that his purpose here was to persuade Jessica to marry him, not to figure her out. Damn good thing, too, because the better he got to know her, the more she puzzled him. She'd been willing to risk her own safety for the sake of a stray mutt, but her grandfather's feelings and wishes didn't seem to concern her in the slightest.

With a shrug, Ryan turned his attention to the fireplace. Luckily his inability to understand her didn't interfere with the edgy desire he'd done his best to ignore since she'd melted in his arms.

Before this evening was over, he fully intended to kiss her again, and more than once—unless she objected. What happened after that was up to her, just as long as she agreed to become his wife.

After he'd finished talking to his protégé, Stuart Walker set down his cordless phone and stared out the window of his den to the heated pool that shimmered below. Until recently it had been his habit to swim each evening, regardless of the season, but lately he didn't have the energy for it.

He was getting old, he realized as he breathed in the perfumed air from the extensive gardens that surrounded the main building. He'd been right to start putting his life in order, just in case. Of far more importance to him than the vast business he'd built from nothing or the wealth that had come with success, and certainly more important than this pile of brick in which he lived, was the one remnant he had of his son—his only grandchild, Jessica.

Stuart had always been a man who planned each step of his life, dotting each *i* and crossing every *t*. Surely he could be forgiven for wanting to see Jessica settled and her future secure, as well as that of his empire and its employees?

In Ryan Noble, he'd chosen his successor well, but the call Stuart had just received was frustrating in its lack of concrete information. All his young associate would say was that Jessica was fine, things were progressing and for Stuart not to worry.

Not worry? If it hadn't been for a stroke of luck, Jessica would even now be married to some small-town nobody who had no more capacity to appreciate her position than did the horse that had thrown her the last time she'd gone riding. Luck was for gamblers and fools.

As progress reports went, Ryan's call had left too many gaps, the signal failing before Stuart could voice his questions. He hadn't been looking for a damn weather report; what he wanted was to hear she had agreed to forget whatever nonsense had sent her away in the first place and accepted Ryan's proposal.

How difficult was that?

Despite Deidre's assurances to the contrary, Stuart knew Jessica regarded him as an interfering old man. Who could blame her? He'd hardly been the father figure she'd needed growing up. He'd been too busy expanding his business. Lately he'd tried to amend that, with varying degrees of success.

He'd been gratified to discover that her mother hadn't managed to turn Jessica into a clone of herself. Although he'd tolerated Deidre's position as his son's widow for all these years, he considered her a parasite. If it hadn't been for Jessica, he would have paid Deidre off and sent her packing long ago.

Well aware of her fondness for the good things in life, and much better informed about the background from which she'd clawed her way up than she knew, he would continue to tolerate her presence as long as she did right by the one link that bound them—Jessica. Deidre had guaranteed him that she would bring about the joining of his sole heir and the only other person he had ever allowed himself to care about since Lawrence died.

Stuart's hands tightened on the windowsill. He was well aware that Deidre considered the marriage between Ryan and Jessica a means to strengthen her own position in the Walker hierarchy, just as he was aware that Jessica's disappearance had frightened Deidre as much as it did him.

The girl had exhibited a rebellious streak he

couldn't help but admire. Nevertheless, he had no intention of condoning her behavior. She would fulfill his wishes and marry Ryan or he would cut her—and her mother—out of his will with a mere fraction of his estate. Knowing Deidre and her greed, he had no doubt she would do everything in her power to convince Jessica to cooperate.

After they'd eaten and Sarah had taken a warm shower while Ryan called Willow Springs, she waited restlessly for him to finish his turn in the bathroom and join her in front of the fire. The intensity of his stare when she'd appeared wearing his robe had told her more than words that he hadn't forgotten what had happened between them earlier.

Well, neither had she. Nervously she crossed to the window, wrapping her arms around her waist, and looked outside. The moon had risen, its pale light leaching the color from the landscape and turning it into a study in contrasts, like a black-and-white photograph. The starkness made Sarah shiver despite the fire, and to feel alone despite Quincy's prone form asleep on his blanket in the corner.

She was so glad he was all right, and she couldn't forget Ryan's tenderness and understanding toward man's best friend. His consideration gave her hope. If he could care about the fate of a stray, he was more than capable of the emotions he professed to distrust.

A noise distracted her from her thoughts, and she looked up to see Ryan leaning against the doorjamb with his thumbs hooked into the waistband of black jeans that rode low on his hips. He'd shaved and his hair was freshly washed. Since she was wearing his robe, he'd put on a dark red shirt he hadn't bothered to button. His gaze was hooded, his expression unreadable. As Sarah stared, a muscle jumped in his cheek.

Anything half as dangerous as he looked right now should have come with a warning label. Her ability to form words was washed away by a tide of lust that shocked her with its intensity. As he came toward her, it wasn't so much that she stood her ground as that her feet had become welded to the floor.

He didn't stop until he was so close that his bare chest nearly brushed against her breasts. Her eyes widened and she trembled, one hand clutching the lapels of the oversized robe as if it were a lifeline. For a long silent moment he searched her face while she wondered what he hoped to see. Then he shifted, and her pulse leaped with anticipation as she expected him to haul her into his arms. Instead he extended his hand, palm up.

Sarah stared down at it, her mind blank. Slowly, as he continued to wait, understanding dawned. She slid her palm against his as his fingers curled around hers. The gesture seemed to say, *we're in this together.* Then he tugged lightly, pulling her toward him as her gaze flew back to his face.

Slightly off-balance, she had to release her grip on the robe so she could brace her hand against the bare, hot skin of his chest. His eyes darkened at her touch and she felt his indrawn breath.

"If you don't want this as much as I do," he said in a low, hoarse voice, "tell me now because I guarantee that in another few moments nothing short of a heart attack is going to stop me from taking you."

A bubble of hysteria rose in Sarah's throat. Her lips parted, but no sound came out.

His gaze narrowed. "Jessica? What's wrong?"

She ignored the way being called by someone else's name made her feel. She'd dealt with that decision already. "Nothing's wrong," she squeaked, her fingers spreading against the hard wall of his chest. This wasn't the time to confess her inexperience. From what he'd just announced about his intentions, he'd know soon enough.

Chapter Eight

Ryan sincerely hoped he hadn't overestimated the strength of his control when he'd given Jessica a last chance to say no before scooping her into his arms and heading for the bedroom. He wasn't quite sure just where persuasion, seduction and staking a claim had gotten muddled up together, but he suspected it had begun the first time he'd kissed her.

All he knew for sure was if she turned him down it would take every ounce of his resolve to back away. When Deidre had first pointed her daughter out to him across a crush of people, he'd figured making Jessica his bride was a straightforward way to repay Stuart for his support and guidance as well as gaining a beautiful wife. What Ryan hadn't counted on was this *need* to make her his in the most basic way that mattered.

Need wasn't supposed to enter the mix at all.

Now Ryan stood gripping her hand like a supplicant, afraid to let go as he searched her face for some clue to her feelings. What he saw there was more than mere acceptance. In her slumberous eyes and her softly parted lips he read a sweetly feminine response to the passion roaring through his own body, as well as a hint of nervousness in the fingers that trembled in his and something else in her expression he couldn't define.

"I've never wanted anyone the way I do you," he admitted, knowing every word was true.

She lifted her chin, her gaze steady. "Show me how much."

It was all the encouragement Ryan needed. He gathered her into his arms, cradling her close as she pressed one hand to his bare chest. The neckline of her borrowed robe gaped open, the glimpse of her breasts affecting him as if he were an adolescent at the window of the girls' locker room. The blood drained from his head so fast it left him rock-hard and slightly dizzy. His grip on her tightened.

"What's wrong?" she asked as she looped her arms around his neck. The movement deepened the curve of her cleavage.

Ryan sucked in a breath, ignoring his body's reaction. "Nothing." His voice sounded thin to his ears as his gaze met her anxious one. "I'll take good care of you." With a glance at the fireplace to make sure the fire was burning down, he carried her from the room.

"I know you will," Sarah told him, glorying in the easy strength with which he carried her.

Was it possible he could be nervous? She'd figured a man like Ryan had plenty of experience to draw on, but she didn't want to dwell on the kind of beautiful, skilled women who must have shared his bed before her. None of them could have felt about him the way Sarah did now.

For the time being, her love would be enough—that and the smoldering gleam in his gaze when he looked down at her. He'd said he wanted her. She knew the hours with him were numbered unless she could convince him a loveless union was a huge mistake. This was her chance, her one shot.

She didn't allow herself to believe that she resembled his intended enough to deceive Jessica's family. The woman's grandfather might have been fooled by a grainy newspaper photo, but the charade was going to be over when he saw Sarah in the flesh.

What would Ryan do then? Could Sarah put aside her own nervousness and show him how important he'd become to her in the short time they'd spent together? Would it make a difference?

When he pushed open the door to the bedroom, she could barely contain a gasp of surprise. It must have been while she was in the shower that he'd started a fire in the woodstove, because the room was pleasantly warm, but that wasn't what brought tears of appreciation to her eyes.

Candles were scattered all around, turning the rustic room into a romantic retreat. The covers on the bed had been turned down invitingly, reminding Sarah that she'd soon be sharing it with the rogue who'd stolen her heart. Her nerves fluttered like butterflies. What if he was disappointed in her?

He stood in the doorway, still holding her in his arm. "Do you like it?" he asked in a low voice, watching her closely. "I would have left a rose on the pillow, but fresh flowers are in short supply around here. Even the red blooms of the local snow plants are covered."

She'd been right; he was nervous, too. Sarah tangled her fingers in the silken strands of hair at his nape. "I don't need flowers and I love the candles," she said huskily. She wanted to add that she loved him, as well, but she was afraid the words would spook him.

All he was looking for was a merger, she reminded herself as he crossed to the bed and set her on her feet beside it. He'd made it clear how he felt about letting his emotions get involved. He wanted no part of that.

If she had a prayer of changing his mind, she wasn't going to do it by talking. She started to undo the tie belt on her robe, but he stopped her by covering her hands with his.

"Let's take it slow," he suggested softly as he traced a path up her arms to her shoulders and gave them a squeeze before he cupped her face, his touch gentle.

Sarah looked deep into his eyes. Could he tell how inexperienced she was? Did it show? Was she being clumsy? Inept? Not if the color running up his cheekbones was any indication, or the hard line of his mouth or the way his pupils had expanded. His features were stamped with stark need. Even she could tell that he desired her. When she leaned into him, aligned against his muscular frame, she was sure of it.

This time when he pressed his lips to hers, he took his time. When he finally let her go, Sarah was afraid her legs might not hold her upright.

Underlying the skill and passion of the kiss was an aching tenderness that stirred a response deep inside her. No matter what happened once they left this wilderness haven, she was going to savor every moment they spent here together.

Instead of removing her robe, Ryan took the time to tuck her hair behind her ear and skimmed his fingertips down the side of her throat, scrambling her pulse. Slowly he undid the belt at her waist.

''Beautiful,'' he murmured, baring her shoulder and bowing his head to nibble a trail of fire across her sensitive skin as her bones turned to water. She hardly noticed when the robe slid down to land in a heap at her feet. Ryan's gaze followed, warm approval in his eyes as she stood before him without a stitch on.

It took an effort to keep her hands at her sides instead of attempting to cover herself. Not even Dan had seen this much of her.

"You're lovely." Ryan's voice was hoarse, his smile slightly crooked.

It was nice of him to say that. Sarah knew she had an average body, not thin and not fat, and she was way too pale. From what she could see through the gap in his unbuttoned shirt, though, Ryan's bronze form was far from average. She glimpsed a wide chest dusted with dark hair. A narrow strip of it crossed his flat stomach and disappeared into his jeans.

Without thinking, she pressed her hand against that intriguing patch between his flat male nipples, surprised at the springy texture. He sucked in a breath, chest expanding, and she dropped her hand.

"Don't stop," he whispered harshly, and then he stripped off his shirt. "Touch me as much as you want."

A muscle jumped in his cheek and she became aware that he had to be holding himself severely in check. Determined to unleash the raw hunger she saw in his eyes, she did what he suggested. Slowly she smoothed her palms up his chest to his wide shoulders, exploring each swell of hard, masculine muscle. The action brought her bare breasts close enough to accidentally brush against him.

He groaned and his hands fisted at his sides. Intrigued, she repeated the movement, watching his jaw clench. The teasing contact puckered her nipples and sent sparks through her body.

Ryan cupped her breasts and bent his head. The touch of his lips on her sensitized flesh exploded through her and she moaned, her head falling back as she clutched at his shoulders. He straightened, burying one hand in her hair, and captured her mouth in a burning kiss. His flesh was hot, his jeans rough as his arousal pressed against her. Sensation after sensation spilled through her as they touched and clung.

Without her realizing quite how it happened, she found herself lying across the huge bed. Ryan stripped off the rest of his clothes before he joined her, looming over her like a sensual predator as his hooded gaze locked with hers.

This was what the fuss was all about, she thought hazily as Ryan's mouth worked its magic, and then his hand scorched a path down her body and she forgot to think at all.

As he stroked her intimately, Ryan knew he was dangerously close to losing control. She was moist and trembling. He managed one more heated kiss and then he parted her legs with his knee. For an instant she stiffened, and he wondered if he'd misread her. Then she wrapped her arms and her legs around him, and it was too late for hesitation. Pure male instinct took over as he claimed her, and then shock stilled him like a bucket of snow.

His eyes flew open. "You—" he rasped, stunned by his discovery. Before his sluggish brain could find the words and his tongue form them, she arched against him.

"Ryan, please," she gasped, the need in her voice shattering the last dregs of his control.

Unable to resist the blatant invitation, he thrust once and then again, barely registering the flare of surprise in her eyes. His own fulfillment rushed toward him. Somehow he managed to hold back until he felt the ripple of her climax, heard her sweet exclamation, and then he let go completely.

Afterwards, Ryan cradled her close and pressed a gentle kiss to her hair. She could nearly feel the question he didn't voice as her heartbeat and breathing slowed to a semblance of normal.

Why had she made him her first?

"Are you all right?" he asked instead.

He'd rolled over so that she was sprawled across him like a rag doll. Her cheek rested against his chest and one leg was flung across his thigh.

"Mmm," she managed. "I'm just lovely." In truth she felt as though a giant wave had rolled her over and over until she thought her lungs would burst, and then tossed her up on the beach like a handful of flotsam.

Beneath her, the beach shifted. She felt his gaze on her. Her eyes flew open as he propped himself against the pillows, one arm around her shoulders. His smile was, if anything, both tender and possessive.

"What about you?" she asked daringly, needing the words. "Was I...okay?"

A chuckle rumbled up from his chest and his arm tightened. "More than okay. I'd say we're a hundred percent compatible."

Relief washed through her, followed by a rush of purely feminine exultation. Feeling empowered, she smoothed her fingers over his chest, tickling the hair, circling his nipples. She scraped him lightly with her nails and watched his reaction.

"Can we do it again?" she whispered, astonished at her own boldness.

"You're not too sore?" Already, as she shook her head, he was turning, dragging her against him. His mouth closed over hers, his hands claiming her with a possession that fired her senses even as his kiss did. Once again they soared together, convincing her without a doubt the first time had been no fluke.

Afterwards Ryan blew out the candles and then he gathered Sarah close. She woke again to the sounds of him stoking the woodstove.

"You could have tipped me off," he pointed out mildly after he'd slid back under the covers and tucked one arm beneath his head. "I might have done things a little differently."

She scooted to a sitting position, studying his profile in the dim light reflected from the snow outside and wishing she could tell what he was thinking.

He'd been a caring teacher and she was a fast learner. Her body still hummed pleasantly from their earlier lovemaking and he gave every indication of being as content as a lion after a feast.

"I didn't know how to tell you," she replied, ducking her head. "I suppose most women my age know what they're doing when it comes to..." Her voice trailed off and she bit her lip. How did she tell him that, until now, she'd been content to wait?

"It hadn't occurred to me that you were still a virgin," he admitted, "but don't think for a minute that being a woman's first lover is some kind of burden.'' He took her hand in his and brought it to his mouth. ''It's a gift,'' he said softly after he'd nibbled on her knuckles, ''one any man would be a fool not to appreciate. I just assumed that you and the guy back at the church—''

''You mean Dan,'' she interjected.

''Well, I'm glad you never did.'' His eyes seemed to glitter in the dim light. ''I hope I wasn't too rough.'' His voice had taken on a husky edge. ''I usually have more control.''

She didn't want to think what that ''usually'' implied. She knew he'd been with other women, plenty of them, but his admission meant he'd wanted her more. Impulsively she laid her hand against his cheek, savoring the warmth and the slight roughness from his whiskers, sprouted since he'd shaved earlier.

''I'll never forget tonight,'' she said.

''Me, either.'' He glanced at the window. ''Tonight is nearly over, though. Dawn's not far away.''

Sarah smothered a yawn. ''Do you think we'll have any more snow?''

''It's getting pretty late in the season. I didn't expect this last storm, so obviously I'm no expert,'' he replied.

She hid another yawn behind her hand. Sometime during the night Quincy had come in to curl up on the red-and-black rug near the woodstove. The rest of the cabin was no doubt pretty chilly, but the bed was warm and Sarah was getting drowsy.

''We'd better get some sleep,'' Ryan said, dropping

a kiss onto her mouth before he slid down onto his back and tucked the covers around her. "If it doesn't snow again, the road might be clear enough to drive out of here by afternoon. I'm sure your mother and grandfather will be excited to see you, especially after your abrupt departure." Cuddling Sarah close, he wished her good-night.

Long after his muscles had gone slack and his breathing evened out, Sarah lay in the darkness. She stared at the window, thinking about what he'd said and all it implied. Either he assumed that since she'd slept with him she was now willing to marry him, or he no longer cared about that. Either way, for Sarah the oblivion of sleep was a long time coming.

Ryan was awakened by the feel of Quincy's cold nose against his arm. When he cracked open his eyes, the dog ran to the door of the bedroom and back again, his meaning unmistakable. Careful not to disturb Jessica, Ryan slipped out of bed and donned the bathrobe she'd borrowed the night before as Quincy bolted from the room.

After Ryan turned off the alarm, he let Quincy out the front door. "Don't you go chasing any rabbits this time or you'll have to find your own way back," Ryan warned.

There was no way he'd leave Jessica to wake up alone, not today. The trees were already dripping as the snow melted and there was no reason to stay any longer.

No practical reason.

As much as he would have liked staying holed up here one more night, he assumed she'd be ready to face Deidre and Stuart. No doubt the business needed Ryan's attention, as well. He hadn't planned on being out of touch. Still, the images of making love on the rug in front of a roaring fire, away from the world's distractions, of getting to know her better over a meal they'd fixed together with no phone to interrupt, certainly had their appeal.

Besides, technically she hadn't yet agreed to marry him, but after she'd given him her virginity last night he didn't doubt that she would. He got hard just thinking of her naked body snuggled under the down quilt right now, waiting for him to join her.

He wished the dog would hurry up.

Jessica's scent, the smell of her hair, her taste and the way she melted when Ryan touched her all managed to turn him inside out with desire. He wanted more of what they'd shared, but he was afraid she would be sore, so he would have to be patient.

He couldn't recall the last time he'd been this needy. Perhaps being snowed in together had skewed his senses, but once they got back to civilization he would surely be able to get this whole relationship thing back into perspective.

Quincy finally returned to shake melting snow all over Ryan's bare feet, then went to the kitchen for a drink of water. Ryan considered calling Stuart. He got as far as opening his briefcase and picking up the phone before he decided he'd better talk to Jessica first, just to make sure they were on the same page.

He'd stayed away from his bride-to-be for long enough, he thought with a private grin. It was time she woke up.

Sarah had no idea what time she'd finally fallen asleep, but when she opened her eyes it was light out and she was alone. For a moment she wondered whether she'd dreamed the night before, but the imprint of Ryan's head was still on the pillow next to hers and the remains of all the candles he'd burned were still scattered around the room. The only thing that was missing, she realized when she sat up and swung her bare legs over the side of the bed, was her robe.

Of course it wasn't really hers, but it was the only thing she had to put on besides something else of Ryan's. How she wished she had some of the pretty lingerie from her luggage to save her from dashing to the bathroom in the shirt he'd had on last night.

After they left here, they'd have to stop in Bellville so she could pick up a few things. She had no intentions of facing the Walkers wearing her wrinkled wedding dress and one shoe.

Guiltily she thought of Dan and his family as she hurried back to the bedroom, pulled off the flannel shirt and scooted into the warm bed. How was her former fiancé handling her apparent desertion?

Despite the letter she'd inadvertently left behind, his family and some of her other friends might be concerned by her continued absence. Did they all hate her? Was Dan's sister furious with her? Sarah would have to borrow Ryan's cell phone to call them, even though she was far from ready to deal with anything outside her new relationship with Ryan.

"You're awake," he said, startling her. A possessive smile curved his mouth.

She'd been so engrossed in thought that she hadn't been aware of his reappearance. A tingle went through her at the sight of him standing in the doorway, his dark hair still mussed from sleep and his eyes hooded. The green robe, she decided, looked much better on him.

"Where were you?" she asked.

Quincy appeared next to Ryan, tail wagging. "I had to let the dog out," Ryan explained as Quincy approached the bed and laid his head on the quilt next to Sarah's hand. His brown eyes stared up at her with silent entreaty.

Sarah patted his silky fur and scratched behind his ears while she told him what a good dog he was. Satisfied, he padded back out of the room.

Perhaps she should feel awkward with Ryan, considering everything they'd done last night, but she didn't. Not after the way he had treated her, as if she were the only woman in his world.

"How are you this morning?" she asked softly as the sheet slid down until it barely covered her breasts. As she reached to pull it back up, she noticed the way Ryan's gaze had shifted, his cheeks darkening as his jaw clenched. Her hands went still.

Quickly he crossed to the bed, leaning over to brace

his arms on either side of her as his gaze pinned her against the pillows.

"Good morning," he replied, voice gravelly. "I hope you didn't plan on getting up right away."

He bent his head and gave her a searing kiss as Sarah snaked her arms around his neck. When he was done, it was all she could do to keep from squirming with the fresh need he aroused in her so effortlessly.

Before she could collect her thoughts, he gently loosed her hold on him. Stripping off the robe, he joined her beneath the covers, but not before she noticed that his magnificent body was heavily aroused.

It was close to midmorning by the time she stirred in Ryan's arms, her eyelids fluttering open as her full mouth softened in a smile. He'd been watching her for some time. Waking up next to her every morning would be no hardship, he realized with a jolt of awareness.

Somehow she'd managed to slip beneath his defenses and touch the part of him he kept carefully guarded. He wasn't sure how he felt about that, but by the time they'd dressed and were seated across the breakfast table from each other, he had managed to reassure himself that he could enjoy a union with Jessica and still keep his emotions under control as long as he was careful. It was either that or risk ending up a slave to his feelings, like his mother had been to hers.

All it would take was discipline.

He was watching Jessica over the rim of his coffee mug while she chatted about some movie she'd seen recently. For someone with the privileged background she had enjoyed, her tastes seemed remarkably uncomplicated; popular music rather than classical, films over opera, and an apparent lack of interest in art or antiques. Not that Ryan was an opera fan—give him a good action movie any day—or that different interests mattered all that much. Not compared to the way she had responded to him last night. Some shared interests were definitely more important than others.

"Let's take a walk when we're done here," he suggested, figuring it might be easier to talk about the wedding while they were outside. He'd found on other occasions that the pure mountain air tended to clear his head, and the majestic Douglas firs reminded him of his relative insignificance in the order of the universe. "I'd like you to see the area when we're not tramping through a storm. It's really lovely."

Jessica's expression relaxed, and he wondered what had put the strain on her face. Perhaps she was reluctant to face her grandfather, but she had to know he'd forgive her anything.

"I'd like that," she replied.

"I'm sorry we don't have more comfortable boots for you, but we won't be in a hurry this time."

For a moment she toyed with the handle of her coffee cup. "Could I use your cell phone?" she asked. "I need to call someone in Bellville and let them know I'm okay."

Instantly Ryan realized he should have offered to let her use the phone sooner. How awkward if anyone had reported her alter ego missing. Then a sudden suspicion made him consider her through narrowed eyes.

Would she have slept with him just so he would let down his guard? The idea was so ludicrous that he nearly laughed.

"Of course you can use it. I'm sure some of your friends must be worried sick." He refused to consider what her former fiancé must be going through.

"Actually, they're probably not," she replied, pleating the napkin beside her plate. "You see, I'd written Dan a letter and I must have dropped it when I fainted."

Ryan leaned forward on his elbows. "What kind of letter would keep people from wondering what had happened to you?"

"One telling him I had changed my mind about marrying him." Her cheeks were pink, her gaze edged with anxiety. "I'm sure everyone thinks I ran out on him, but I never intended for him to see what I wrote."

"Why not?" Ryan asked, confused. "And why did you change your mind?"

She looked down at her hands. "I didn't want to hurt Dan, but I was starting to suspect that my feelings for him weren't what they should have been."

A surge of possessiveness caught Ryan by surprise. Feelings had nothing to do with it, unless you counted her desire to rebel against her family's wishes.

She cleared her throat. "You kept me from making a big mistake. I know that now and I want to thank you."

It was his turn to look away. "No thanks necessary." He assumed she was referring to his role in stopping her wedding.

"Don't you want to know why I'm so sure I didn't love Dan enough to be his wife?" she persisted softly.

Maybe she was about to save Ryan from having to ask some awkward questions, like did she intend to marry him when they got back to Willow Springs. "Why don't you tell me why."

"Because I've fallen in love with you."

Her words hung in the air between them while he gaped at her, too stunned to speak. Part of him knew she was waiting for him to say something in return, but before he could articulate a reply, the moment passed, followed by an awkward silence he had no idea how to fill.

"Jessica—" he croaked, horrified to see the hurt in her eyes. "I don't—"

Before he could admit that he didn't know what to say, there was a sudden pounding on the door, followed immediately by Quincy's wild barking.

Jessica's glistening eyes went wide with surprise. "Were you expecting anyone?"

Ryan shoved back his chair and got to his feet. "Not unless your grandfather got tired of waiting and sent a posse after us." Who else would have braved the bad roads? "Uh, I'd better see who it is," he added lamely, feeling like a coward to be so pathetically relieved by the interruption.

"Be careful." Her warning came as a surprise, but

a nice one, considering how he must have just plummeted to the bottom of her favorite guy list.

Seeing the anxiety on her face, he paused long enough to dig a heavy crescent wrench out of the drawer and stuck it in his back pocket. Before he could tell her to stay put, she sidled up to the front window and peeked out.

"There's a Bronco parked by your Jeep with a rack of lights on top and some kind of official insignia on the door," she said in a stage whisper. "What shall we do?"

How the hell had they found out she was here? Would she still press charges if she loved him?

"I guess I'd better see what they want." He glanced through the window and sagged with relief. At least it wasn't a SWAT team waiting outside with guns drawn and tear gas canisters at the ready.

"I know this guy," he told Jessica. Her face was pale, but he didn't have time to wonder why. The insistent pounding came again, followed by more barking from Quincy, as Ryan hastily deactivated the alarm.

"It's okay," Jessica murmured to the excited setter, patting his head while Ryan opened the door.

"Craig, what are you doing here?" he asked the officer standing in front of him in a bulky uniform jacket and khakis, a holstered gun on his hip. "Is something wrong?"

The deputy glanced at Jessica and nodded politely before he returned his attention to Ryan. "Sorry to disturb you two," he said with a knowing look on his face. "I saw the smoke from your chimney. I just wanted to make sure you didn't get caught unprepared by the storm like a few other people around here did. Everything okay?"

Ryan held his breath on the off chance Jessica would still take this opportunity to get away from him. Had she meant what she'd just said, or was it part of some elaborate plan of escape?

When she didn't immediately expose him as a criminal, he slid his arm around her waist possessively and introduced her. Did she find Craig attractive? Some women went for the uniform and he was big and blond, with a ruddy complexion from spending his life outdoors.

If anything, Jessica seemed uncharacteristically shy, nearly hiding behind Ryan. He felt her tremble as she returned Craig's greeting.

Had she been pulled over for speeding or some other infraction that had made her wary of the police? Perhaps she was just concerned that her privacy would be compromised. No doubt she'd been a victim of the press before, but Ryan could reassure her that Craig was a stand-up guy who didn't leak juicy tidbits to the gossip rags.

The deputy tipped his hat. "You both okay?" he asked.

"Of course," Jessica replied rather forcefully. "We're fine, aren't we?" She glanced up at Ryan for confirmation.

"No problem," he agreed. "How's the main

road?'' he asked Craig. ''We're thinking about heading out a little later.''

''There are a few slushy spots, but you should be fine if you go before dark.'' The deputy bent down and stretched out his hand for Quincy to sniff. ''I didn't know you had a dog.''

Briefly Ryan explained how they'd acquired the Irish Setter. ''Has anyone reported one lost?''

Craig straightened. ''Not that I've heard, but I'll keep my ears open and I'll let you know if I hear anything. Well, I'll be going now.''

''Would you like a cup of coffee?'' Ryan asked reluctantly. He didn't want to give up a minute alone with Jessica, but it had been good of Craig to come by.

For a moment, that unprofessional gleam reappeared in the other man's gaze. ''Naw, I've got a couple other places to check on, but thanks.'' He glanced back at Jessica and touched the brim of his hat again. ''Ma'am. Enjoy the rest of your stay, and if this bum gives you any trouble, just call nine-one-one and I'll be here with cuffs and a rubber hose.''

''Okay,'' she replied. ''Thanks.''

After more goodbyes, Ryan watched the deputy return to his vehicle and drive away with a last wave.

Sarah watched the deputy leave with a sigh of relief. Yesterday she would have welcomed a lawman, but today was a different story. She'd been scared to death he was going to blow her cover by announcing that he was here to take her, Sarah Daniels, back to Bellville and arrest Ryan for kidnapping. Now that she was able to think rationally again, she realized if that were the case, he wouldn't have come alone.

She'd been so busy worrying that he would expose her that she hadn't given a thought to telling him the truth. Like the old song said, what a difference a day made.

"Mind telling me why you were acting like you got caught red-handed?" Ryan asked after he'd shut the front door. "The last person I saw act so nervous around a cop had been embezzling from one of my companies."

"Are you implying that I've been stealing your silver?" Sarah demanded, feigning indignation. "You're welcome to frisk me." Holding out her arms, she turned slowly around.

To her relief, her ruse seemed to work in distracting him. Catching her in his arms, he buried his face in her hair. "I've got a better idea," he murmured.

Sarah clung to him, her knees weak from the recent scare. "And what is that?" she asked, figuring she knew the answer already.

"Let's take Quincy and go for a walk. There's something I want to discuss with you."

Chapter Nine

Time was running out for Sarah. As she walked through the unbroken snow with Ryan and Quincy, she was painfully aware that even if she continued letting him believe she was Jessica, he'd find out the truth soon enough. Should she confess now and make him listen, risking his rejection, or should she soak up every sweet moment with him and let later take care of itself?

They came to a steep section of the path and Ryan reached for her hand, pulling her close to steal a kiss before he guided her over the rough spot. Returning his smile, seeing the gleam of desire in his eyes, Sarah knew she couldn't give up one minute of the time they had left. She feared the real world was going to intervene soon enough. No reason for her to hold open the door.

They reached a clearing that was bisected by a fallen tree. Tugging her along with him, Ryan went over to the log and brushed off the snow with his free hand.

"Why don't you sit down," he invited, the muscles of his throat working as he swallowed with uncharacteristic nervousness.

Suddenly Sarah didn't think she wanted to hear what he had to say. What if he told her he couldn't return her feelings? Or worse yet, that he now realized she'd been telling the truth at the beginning and she wasn't really his high-society heiress. She couldn't very well lie to him about her identity. Once he knew the truth, he might very well take her back to Bellville and resume his search for Jessica.

How could Sarah give him up, even though technically he had never been hers to keep?

"Um, why don't we keep walking?" she suggested with feigned enthusiasm. "I really want to get a little exercise, don't you?"

"Didn't you hike far enough yesterday when we were searching for Quincy?" he teased, a faint smile softening the intriguing planes of his face. "Come on, humor me. There's something I need to say."

Sarah nibbled on her lower lip. She was powerless to postpone the inevitable. If nothing else was gained by this episode, she hoped he wouldn't make the mistake of marrying without love, no matter who he ended up making his bride. At the very least, he deserved a woman who felt about him as Sarah did, but how had she managed to delude herself that a man like Ryan might fall for a country mouse like her, and in only a couple of days? If his expertise in bed was any indication, he'd probably slept with a lot of women without falling in love with them.

"Okay," she agreed reluctantly, allowing him to escort her to the log. Eyes downcast, she perched on it gingerly and folded her hands in her lap. When he didn't speak, she stole a peek at his face. As she looked up, he startled her by going down on one knee and taking her gloved hand in his.

He cleared his throat while Sarah goggled at him.

"What are you doing?" she blurted, although any fool could see exactly what he was about to do.

Panic welled up inside her. How was she supposed to bear this—a marriage proposal from the man who had stolen her heart—without shattering into a thousand pieces? It wasn't *her* he was really asking, after all.

While she stared at his bent head, he placed a kiss on the back of her hand and then he leaned forward to rub his cheek against her glove, like a big jungle cat seeking approval. Vision blurring, she traced the line of his jaw with her fingertips.

He looked up and something flared in the depths of his eyes. "I hope those are happy tears."

Sarah swallowed past the sudden lump in her throat and managed a shaky nod. Who could blame her for wanting to pretend this moment was truly hers, to make a memory she could keep forever? She would have precious few memories of this man with whom she'd spent so little time.

"I admit that we started out on shaky ground," he said, "but I'm confident we can make a go of it. You know what I'm about to ask, so there's no point in rambling on. Will you do me the honor of becoming my wife?"

Sarah stared at him, imprinting every detail of his face, every nuance of his expression, in her mind. With his cheeks reddened by the cold and his hair falling across his forehead, he'd never looked more handsome.

Instead of the arrogance she might have expected, she saw instead a glimmer of uncertainty in his gray eyes. She could imagine his smile were she to tell him what he wanted to hear. Once she accepted, he would be eager to leave. If she refused, would he keep her here longer, using every means he had to persuade her, every sensuous trick in his arsenal of expertise, or would his patience finally run out?

"I'm not sure," she compromised, stalling for time.

His smile faded as his hand tightened on hers before he released it. "You've admitted that you love me," he replied, his voice edged with exasperation. "It's more than some couples start out with, so what's not to be sure about?"

"Your feelings for me." She nearly forgot she was supposed to be playing a part. She knew better than to expect—

"I'm not good at emotions," he replied, touching

her cheek, "but I can promise that as long as we're married, I'll be faithful to you in every way and I'll never deliberately do anything to hurt or embarrass you."

Sarah turned her head away. *As long as we're married,* he'd said. The idea that he didn't expect it to be permanent should have made it easier for her to let him go now, but it didn't.

Gently he captured her chin and urged her to meet his gaze. "Jessica," he said, sending a shaft of pain through her so fierce that it stole her breath, "I know I can't force you to believe me, but I have to tell you that my reasons for wanting you to become my wife have changed since I first saw you at that church."

Sarah could hardly absorb what he was saying. Did he love her, after all? "What do you mean?" she asked breathlessly.

Ryan got to his feet, pulling her up with him. "It's true that I mean to fulfill Stuart's wishes," he said, holding her hands in his, "and to cement our business partnership, but there's something else I want, as well."

"What's that?" Despite what he'd said earlier, she was beginning to hope that miracles happened after all.

"I don't want to lose you." His voice was husky. "We've started something between us, something I want to explore. I figure getting to know you will take at least the next fifty years, if we're lucky." He chuckled softly. "As much as it terrifies me to admit it, I've fallen for you in a big way. So how about it? Will you say yes?''

Sarah looked into his eyes, drowning in what she saw there, and took the chance that somehow, love would triumph. ''Yes, Ryan, I'll marry you.''

As soon as the words were out and he swept her into his arms, she realized she had just brought an end to their idyll. It was her last coherent thought before his mouth covered hers and he took her under.

Reluctantly Ryan broke the kiss, surprised at the feelings that had poured through him when she said yes. He'd expected the same sense of relief, even triumph, that he experienced when a deal came together, but this time the intensity of his emotions was a surprise and not an entirely pleasant one. He felt as though he were white-water rafting with no paddle, and situations beyond his control made him nervous.

''Let's close up the cabin and get out of here,'' he suggested a little more sharply than he'd intended. ''I want to share our news, and I'm sure you're eager to see your mother and grandfather.''

''Actually I was hoping we could go to Bellville first and pick up a few things,'' Jessica responded. ''I can't very well show up in my wedding dress and bare feet, and my car is there, too.''

''You won't need your car for a couple of days and you must have a bedroom full of clothes at the house,'' he countered, disliking the idea of returning to the scene of her near-marriage to another man. Possessiveness was new to him. ''Can't Bellville wait?''

"I know it's out of our way, but I still need shoes," she replied. "Please?"

As impatient as he was to give Stuart their news, Ryan found that denying her anything as long as her big blue eyes were pleading with him was more than he could do. So much for control.

"Sure," he said with a shrug. "As soon as we get back to the cabin I'll call Stuart and tell him we're more or less on our way."

Her smile was ample reward for the detour. When they reached the cabin, he picked up the cell phone. Then he turned back to Jessica. "Did you want to let anyone know you're okay?"

She hesitated, biting her lip. "I suppose I'd better." Her voice was flat, making Ryan feel guilty for putting her in such an awkward position in the first place. If only he'd thought the situation through before he'd made off with her.

If he had, she'd be married to someone else by now.

"Let me switch it on," he said, hitting the power button. As soon as he did, a signal alerted him that he had messages. "I'd better check these, just in case," he explained with an apologetic glance. The first one sent a chill through him.

It's Deidre. Call me the moment you get this.

A second message said the same thing. Ryan's hand trembled as he keyed in the numbers. Luckily, she answered on the first ring.

"I think you should get back here as soon as you can," she told him when he'd identified himself.

"Stuart hasn't been feeling very well and he wants to see you."

"What's wrong with him?" Ryan demanded. As long as he'd known Stuart, the older man's health had been good.

"He insists he's just tired, but I've been trying to persuade him to see the doctor. You know how he is about that."

"Yeah, stubborn." Ryan glanced at his watch. "We're leaving now. We should be there in two or three hours. Maybe the sight of his granddaughter will perk him up."

"I take it your news is good?" Deidre asked.

"We'll talk about it when we get there. Did you want to say anything to Jessica?" He looked up, but she'd disappeared. "I'll have her call you from the road," he amended. After he'd promised to drive carefully, he broke the connection just as Jessica walked into the room with her wedding dress over her arm.

"You could have left that here," he told her with another twinge of jealousy. She was marrying *him*, so why did it matter that she wanted to take the dress with her? "You missed talking to your mother."

"I guess that will keep. How's he doing?"

From her grim expression, Ryan assumed she was still holding a grudge. After she'd left Willow Springs, Deidre admitted to him that Jessica "had issues" with their plans for her.

"Deidre said he hasn't been feeling too well," he told her, "but she insists that it's nothing serious."

"That's good," she said with a surprising lack of emotion. "Has he seen the doctor?"

"You know he hates doctors. I had to tell her we'd come straight there," he said apologetically. "We'll stop on the way and pick up something for you to change into before we get there. Meanwhile you'll have to make do with what you've got on and a pair of my hiking boots."

Jessica's cheeks went pink. "I don't have any money, remember? You left my purse behind."

Relief spilled through him and he pulled her into his arms. Was that why her mood seemed to have plummeted or was she more worried about Stuart than she wanted to let on?

"If money is all that's concerning you, I have to say that as my future bride your credit is good with me."

For a moment Sarah allowed herself the bliss of being in his arms, but then she pulled away, knowing he had to be concerned about the man he was willing to go to such great lengths to please.

In moments their meager belongings were stowed in the Jeep and Ryan had put Quincy's blanket behind the seat. While he closed up the cabin, she took the dog outside for a last rest stop before their long drive.

"It doesn't seem like only two days ago that we got here," Ryan said as he turned the Jeep around and headed down the narrow track through the melting snow.

Quincy had already curled up on his blanket like a seasoned traveler, so apparently he was accustomed to riding in a car. Sarah turned around and watched the cabin through the trees until they went around a bend and it disappeared from sight.

"A lot has happened since our arrival," she replied, recalling how upset she'd been when he'd first brought her here. She had no idea then if he was even completely sane and, if anyone had told her she'd end up falling for him, she would have laughed herself sick.

"Could I use the phone now?" she asked. "There's someone I need to call."

Ryan hit the power button with his thumb and handed it to her. "Sorry I can't give you any privacy."

He must have figured she intended to call Dan, but after what she'd put the poor man through, he deserved more than a phone call. Biting her lip, Sarah punched in Kelly's number, hoping Dan's sister was home. It was a relief to hear her friend's voice.

"Where are you?" Kelly demanded, her tone unfriendly. She had good reason to be upset. "Even after reading that letter you left, Dan's been worried."

"Please tell him that I'm okay and I'm really, really sorry," Sarah replied, hoping she could salvage her friendship with Kelly over time.

At least Dan had never acted as though he was wildly in love with Sarah, she realized now, but that didn't excuse her or mean she hadn't hurt and embarrassed him.

"I'll be back in a day or two to explain," she promised Kelly. Sarah was reluctant to go into a lot of detail that would only confuse Ryan, so she ignored her friend's rapid-fire questions. Instead Sarah pretended to lose the signal, feeling like a coward, and switched off the phone.

"That certainly went well," she muttered.

Ryan glanced at her curiously as she set the cell phone back on the console, but he didn't comment. "Grab a nap if you want," he urged. "I know you didn't get a lot of sleep last night, and I can wake you when we get to the mall this side of Willow Springs."

As tired as she was, Sarah had no intentions of wasting any of her remaining time with him by sleeping through it. "Tell me how you and S—my grandfather—got to be so close," she suggested as she peeled one of the oranges Ryan had brought with them.

"He outbid me on a deal a few years ago," Ryan replied as she handed him an orange segment. "I was pretty upset about it at the time. Looking back, I realized he was a wily old fox and I hadn't done my homework. He deserved to win."

He paused to eat the piece of orange in two bites. "Our paths crossed a few more times. He was my biggest rival, always there when I looked over my shoulder. Then one day he called."

Grinning, Ryan shook his head. "I was pretty full of myself, I guess, and I nearly refused his call, but I was curious. He gave me some information about a company I'd been looking at—I have no idea how he knew. Anyway, he said it wasn't anything he could use, but that I might find it interesting.'' He glanced at Sarah. ''Because of what he told me, I made a lot of money. When I called to thank him, he suggested we get together and talk.''

''And did you?'' Sarah wondered how much of this she was supposed to know already, but since Ryan spoke in generalities, she assumed Jessica wasn't involved in the business.

''Yeah. I didn't like him very much at first, but later he told me I reminded him of himself.'' He shrugged. ''Once I got to know him better, I decided that was a compliment.''

Listening to Ryan talk, Sarah started to understand why he'd been so willing to do Stuart's bidding. The older man had become a father figure to Ryan, who'd grown up without one. She wondered if Stuart was elderly, but she could hardly ask.

''I learned a lot from him,'' Ryan added as he slowed for a curve in the winding mountain road. Although the pavement was mostly clear and wet, there was still a lot of snow on the ground around them. ''Your father's death hit him hard. Too bad you never took an interest in his companies.''

Sarah looked away as panic seized her. She had no idea how to respond. What had he said Jessica did to keep busy? Some kind of volunteer work, she remembered vaguely. Oh, why hadn't she paid closer attention?

''The business seemed so dry,'' she ventured. ''I'd rather work with people than numbers.''

Ryan glanced at her sharply and she thought she'd

put her foot in it with her lame comment, but then he covered her hand with his.

"It's probably just as well. Stuart's pretty traditional in his outlook and, as much as I hate to admit it, I don't think he ever would have been comfortable handing over the reins to a woman, not even his own flesh and blood. Not totally. I always had the impression he pictured you in the same role as your mother."

Since Sarah had no idea what role that was, all she could do was to smile brightly. "Is that right?"

"He'll be pleased," Ryan continued. "You know, I think he's come to regret not spending more time with you when you were younger, even though he'd never admit it now. He's not a man who wastes energy looking back, but he loves you very much."

Well, he could say the word without choking, she thought with a trace of bitterness. Just not when it applied to himself.

She had to think of a way to divert their conversation before she made some slip. Call her unwilling to face the inevitable, but she just wasn't ready to tell Ryan the truth, not when he smiled at her with such blatant desire in his eyes.

"Tell me about your place," she suggested daringly. "Whatever I've heard, I guess I've forgotten."

Hiding her free hand down beside her seat, she crossed her fingers. Surely Jessica would have gotten to know him if he lived on the Walker estate.

"I've got a penthouse on the top floor of The Montclair," he replied.

The what? Sarah did her best to look impressed.

"We'll have to start house-hunting together," he continued. "I know there's nothing else that would compare to what you're used to, but if we can't find a house you like, we'll have one built."

Sarah was hit with such a strong wave of sadness that she had to turn away, but not because she hadn't really thought much until now about Ryan's wealth and success. Blindly she stared out the side window and tried not to picture him and Jessica setting up housekeeping together. Could he go ahead and marry someone else when he found out who Sarah was? Providing, of course, that the missing heiress changed her mind and came home.

"What's wrong?" he asked. "I hope you didn't plan on staying on at the estate. I don't think it would be a good idea."

"Oh, neither do I," Sarah agreed. "Finding our own place will be fun."

"I'm glad you're looking forward to it." Ryan turned on the radio. "We should be able to get some music by now." Soon the strains of a romantic ballad filled the car. "This okay?" he asked.

Sarah nodded, tired of playing a role for which she had no script. If she blurted out the truth, would he understand, or would he merely drop her at the next bus stop like an unwanted parcel?

Along with her main reason to wait, she had to admit to a growing curiosity about the woman Stuart and Ryan had both mistaken her for. Sarah had avoided speculating about Jessica Walker, but she

would certainly like to get a peek at her and draw her
own conclusions about their resemblance before she
was tossed out of the Walker mansion on her ear.

Was there a chance Jessica's mother had given
birth to twins and then for some inexplicable reason
abandoned one at the tiny hospital in Bellville? If she
had, had Jessica's grandfather been privy to the
shameful scheme? There were so many questions
Sarah would like to ask, given her own unknown or-
igins. Although the idea of Jessica's mother giving
away one of her babies was pretty ridiculous, perhaps
Sarah could learn something to shed a little light on
the identity of her biological parents.

All she knew was that shortly after her birth, she'd
been left at the hospital in Bellville with a respiratory
infection. After recovering fully, she had spent several
years in the foster care system until all possible leads
about her background had been exhausted and she
was finally released for adoption to an older couple
right in town.

From the age of five until her parents died within
months of each other, Sarah had been part of a loving
family. She knew now it was that feeling she'd been
trying to replicate by marrying Dan. Her disappearance had certainly hurt him, but the damage could
have been much worse if their wedding had taken
place. Falling for Ryan had taught her the difference
between friendship and love; she could only hope it
was a lesson she could survive having learned.

"Are you hungry?" Ryan asked. "We'll be at that

shopping mall pretty soon and there must be some restaurants there, if you want to grab a bite.''

Sarah didn't think she could choke down any food, but he must be famished. They hadn't eaten since breakfast and it was the middle of the afternoon already. Besides, Quincy would need a walk.

''That's a good idea,'' she replied. ''It shouldn't take too long for me to pick up a few things if there's a supermarket handy.''

She realized her mistake when she saw the expression on Ryan's face. Then he laughed. ''You had me going for a minute. I'll bet you've never shopped in a place like that in your life. Knowing Deidre, she would have never permitted that kind of 'slumming.' Don't worry, though. There's at least one department store and a drugstore, if I remember right. They'll do in a pinch.''

''Do we have the time?'' she asked. ''I know you want to get back to see how S—my grandfather is doing.''

Ryan's gaze narrowed. ''What about you? Don't you want to make sure he's okay?''

''Of course I do,'' she exclaimed, the beginnings of a tension headache stabbing her temples.

Ryan's fingers skimmed her cheek. ''I'm sorry,'' he murmured before he turned his attention back to the road. ''I know things are bound to be a little awkward between you. Don't worry about Stuart holding a grudge. I'd just assumed the situation between you two would be all blown over now that you and I are together, but I suppose you still have some issues to work through with him. Just remember that in his own high-handed way, Stuart was looking out for your best interests.'' Returning his hand to the steering wheel, he sighed. ''He'll be happy to hear our news.''

Sarah could make very little sense out of much of what Ryan had just told her. If he wanted to think she had issues with the old man, let him. After all, if Stuart Walker hadn't sent Ryan after his runaway bride-to-be, Sarah would never have met him. Despite the heartbreak that almost certainly lay ahead, she couldn't regret what they'd shared, and she would never forget the last couple of days if she lived to be a hundred and fifty.

''I'll think about what you said,'' she replied as the road leveled out ahead of them.

Ryan smiled his approval. As they passed a few scattered houses, the traffic grew heavier. Eventually more buildings appeared, closer together.

''Don't worry,'' he assured her. ''We'll make the time to buy whatever you feel that you need.''

Sarah managed not to gawk when they finally got to Willow Springs, but it wasn't easy. Just as she had figured, the area was definitely an affluent one with large homes set back from the divided boulevard they were on, many of the structures shielded from view by privacy fences or tall, neatly trimmed hedges. Others were protected by elaborate gates that allowed glimpses of long driveways, mature trees and star-tlingly green lawns. New houses were scattered among much older ones, all surrounded by acres of gardens and grass.

The architectural mix was definitely eclectic. Despite her mingled resignation and dread, Sarah grew curious about their destination. From what little Ryan had said, she'd gathered it was many years old, but of course beyond that, she knew nothing. How frustrating not to be able to ask any questions!

They were passing an old cemetery surrounded by a tall wrought-iron fence when Ryan pulled the Jeep over under a tree. The temperature had warmed considerably and Sarah was grateful for the simple light-green cotton dress and beige sandals he'd purchased for her earlier.

"Why are we stopping?" she asked as Quincy stood up and pressed his nose to the window. Was there some family significance to the cemetery of which she couldn't possibly be aware?

Ryan turned to her with a smile that bumped up her pulse rate as he slid his arm across the back of her seat. Grumbling lightly about the quality, he'd bought an inexpensive sport shirt to replace the heavy flannel one he'd worn down from the cabin. Although the blue plaid flattered his coloring, Sarah suspected he was more at home in custom tailored suits, silk ties and Egyptian cotton shirts that didn't have little buttons holding down the collar points.

His arm tightened around her shoulders. "Can't a guy stop long enough to kiss his fiancée?" he asked lightly, his tone belied by the intensity of his gaze.

"Any time he wants," Sarah replied breathlessly,

vaguely aware that Quincy was sitting patiently behind them. How she wished they were all three back
at the cabin in their own little world.

She slid her hands around Ryan's neck and shifted
closer. "Let's not go straight to the estate," she suggested impulsively. "We can find a room someplace
and hole up there, just the two of us. And Quincy, of
course. What's one more day?"

Ryan's smile faded into obvious confusion as he
leaned back. "Don't you want to make sure your
grandfather is really all right?" he asked.

Realizing her blunder, Sarah summoned up a coy
smile and batted her eyes. "The idea of kissing you
sent everything else right out of my head," she
breathed, groaning inwardly at such a manipulative
attempt to distract him.

To her surprise, the ego stroke worked and his
smile returned. "I knew there was a reason I'm so
attracted to you," he murmured, curving his fingers
around her nape. The moment his mouth touched
hers, everything else did fly right out of her head and
she gave herself up to the raw sensuality of the moment.

As if he, too, sensed that everything was about to
change, he deepened the kiss. Sarah responded helplessly to the possessiveness and desperation behind
the heat, her heart breaking at the idea of finding the
love of her life and then losing him so quickly. Tears
leaked from beneath her closed lids, trickling down
her cheeks as he finally let her go.

"Honey, what's wrong?" he demanded, gripping

her shoulders. "I didn't mean to worry you. Deidre didn't indicate anything was seriously wrong, remember. She just said Stuart has been under the weather and I figured you'd want to see him."

His words made Sarah feel worse as she brushed at the tear tracks with her fingers.

"I know," she managed, pressing her hand to his cheek. "Will you just remember that I love you?"

He turned his face, placing his mouth against her palm. "I'll make you happy," he vowed.

His heavy lashes screened his gaze, his breath tickling the sensitive skin of her hand. She wanted to lie in his arms one more time, to extract every moment of joy she could. Most of all, she wanted to hear him tell her that he loved her—just once—before she saw the light dim from his gaze as he looked at her. Instead she drew in a steadying breath and clamped down hard on her composure as Ryan turned her hand over in his.

"We'll have to go shopping for an engagement ring first chance we get," he said, lacing his fingers with hers. "I want everyone to know you belong to me. What do you want, a diamond?"

"I've always thought an emerald would be nice," she replied. "It's my birthstone." She grimaced, remembering the way Dan had brushed aside her hints for an engagement ring. Somehow she had to hang on to the belief that she and Ryan had a future together or she'd never survive the next few hours. "But any ring you gave me would be wonderful," she added.

For a moment she thought he was going to kiss her again, but then a car drove by and he blinked as though he, too, had forgotten everything else but the two of them.

"Let's let Quincy stretch his legs for a few minutes," he suggested. They'd given the dog some water and a couple of biscuits they bought before they'd had their own lunch at a gourmet pizzeria, so Ryan dug out a plastic bag and let Quincy out of the Jeep. A few moments later they were on their way again.

Sarah had thought she was prepared for anything as Ryan drove through an open wrought iron gate between two massive redbrick pillars and headed down a long driveway bordered by tall palms and elegant formal gardens. The driveway curved in a lazy circle in front of an imposing two-story brick mansion that looked as though it must have been transported brick by brick from Boston or Philadelphia.

Sarah could barely suppress a gasp of surprise. The house was far grander than anything else she'd seen in Willow Springs, and that was saying a lot.

Ryan parked in front of the main entrance while Sarah tried not to gawk. The lawn was manicured like a putting green, bordered by formal hedges, neatly pruned trees and masses of blooming flowers she didn't bother to identify. As she looked around her, Ryan got out and circled the Jeep to open her door. Quincy jumped out after Sarah, crowding close to her as if he, too, were intimidated by the grandeur of the estate.

A gardener who'd been working close by glanced up and Ryan signaled to him, snapping the leash they'd purchased to Quincy's new collar.

"Ben, would you take Quincy down to the stables and ask Charlie to look after him for us," Ryan called out when the man was in earshot.

"Sure thing, Mister Noble," he replied, wiping his hands on his pants before taking the leash. "Welcome home, Miss Jessica." He tipped his head respectfully.

As soon as Sarah thanked him, amazed that he didn't immediately point to her and shout "fraud," he squatted down and extended a hand to the dog, who sniffed it curiously and then wagged his tail.

"We'll check on Quincy later, okay?" Ryan asked her. "He'll be fine with Charlie's old collie, and you know your mother wouldn't have a dog in the house."

"I'll take good care of him," the man called Ben promised. Sarah managed to nod and smile in reply. She was still trying to deal with the gardener not realizing she was an impostor. *What was really going on here?*

After Ben had led Quincy down another part of the driveway that ran beside the house toward a tennis court and some other buildings, Sarah turned her attention to the front entrance.

At the top of the steps, guarded by a pair of imposing granite lions, were a set of massive pillars framing double doors that had been intricately carved from some dark, elegant wood. Not a speck of dust marred their polished beauty.

Before Sarah could reach for Ryan's hand, one of the doors flew open and a petite, elegantly attired blonde appeared, stopping abruptly on the top step with her hands clasped together. Her dress and jewelry were so simple that Sarah knew they had to have cost a fortune. Her makeup and hair were flawless.

The shock on her face, so fleeting it could have been imagined, was quickly masked by a cool smile of welcome, as Sarah realized that beneath the cosmetics, the woman was considerably older than she first appeared.

Ryan's protective hand settled on Sarah's back as he urged her forward. "Hello, Deidre," he said. "Look who I've brought home."

After a fleeting hesitation, the woman came gracefully down the steps, her gaze riveted as she extended both her hands.

"Welcome back, my darling," she said, capturing Sarah's fingers hard in her icy grip as she leaned forward to kiss the air near Sarah's cheek. Heavy perfume tickled Sarah's nose and she nearly sneezed.

When Deidre straightened, the smile of welcome remained firmly planted on her peach tinted lips, but a warning Sarah couldn't miss burned like a cold flame in her blue eyes.

Unlike Ryan, Stuart, and the gardener, this woman hadn't been fooled by Sarah's appearance for a moment. So why hadn't she immediately denounced her as the impostor both of them knew her to be?

Chapter Ten

Deidre took one more look at the young woman standing before her on the steps in a cheap cotton dress and knew that her worst nightmare had just come true. She glanced at Ryan and tried to gauge how much he knew about the situation. There had been a time when she had let her interest in him show, but he'd been oblivious. Now only years of practice enabled her to maintain her composure when her hand itched to slap his handsome face.

"How's Stuart feeling?" he asked.

Deidre had gotten nowhere in gaining her father-in-law's permission to call the doctor. Stubborn old coot! Right now his health was the least of her problems.

"He's resting," she replied, "but he swears he's feeling better."

"I'm sure the sight of his granddaughter will help." Ryan curled his arm possessively around the young woman's waist and smiled down at her while Deidre seethed. Was this Ryan's idea of a joke?

The sight of this creature was more likely to send Stuart into cardiac arrest, but Deidre wasn't about to let the girl anywhere near him. Until she found out just how much these two knew, she had no choice but to play along.

"Come inside, both of you," she told them, leading the way into the foyer with her head held high. Snapping her fingers, she summoned the maid arranging flowers next to a Remington bronze. Thank God this girl had only come from the agency a few weeks ago and had never actually seen Jessica.

"Juanita, show Mr. Noble to the sunroom and fetch him some coffee. And bring a pot of tea up to Jessica's suite."

She glanced back at Ryan, confident that her inner turmoil was hidden beneath a mask of serenity. "You don't mind if I steal her away for a few minutes, do you?" she asked him. "We have quite a bit to catch up on."

The look on his face when he ogled his companion made Deidre's teeth clench. She wouldn't have allowed herself a shred of jealousy toward her own daughter, but this was not Jessica.

"I understand," he said, kissing the girl's cheek before he released her hand.

"Will you have someone let Stuart know I'm here?" he asked Deidre.

"The moment he wakes up." She glided across the foyer.

"Come, darling," she said over her shoulder, "I'm sure you want to freshen up. Let's have a nice mother-daughter chat." Confident her summons would be obeyed, she ascended the curving staircase with her back ramrod straight.

"Did you have a pleasant drive back from the mountains?" she asked as the young woman joined her.

"It was very nice, thank you." Her voice, so like Jessica's, was strained and her grip on the mahogany banister was so tight that her knuckles gleamed as white as bone.

When they reached the landing, Deidre led the way down the wide hallway to Jessica's rooms in the west wing. She wondered whether this interloper was capable of appreciating the original artwork on the walls, and if she was assessing the opulence of her surroundings. Where the hell had Ryan found her, anyway?

Neither of them spoke until after they got to Jessica's private quarters and Deidre had shut the door firmly behind them. As she sat down in one of a pair of matching chairs and crossed her legs, she barely noticed the rosewood furnishings or the canopy bed Jessica liked so much. Folding her hands together in her lap, Deidre studied the creature standing in front of her. Except for the length of her hair, she was an exact replica of Jessica.

The question was, which replica was she?

"Why don't you start by telling me who you are and why you're impersonating my daughter," Deidre demanded.

Sarah stared at the woman seated before her, blond hair styled in a twist, chin angled as regally as a queen holding court. Sarah's instincts told her if she allowed Jessica's mother to walk all over her, she would never find out anything. Deliberately she sat down in the other chair, willing her hands not to tremble nor her voice to shake.

"My name is Sarah Daniels," she said quietly as she held Deidre's gaze. "When Ryan abducted me from my wedding, I told him he had the wrong woman, but he didn't believe me. From what he said and from the photo he showed me of Jessica, I got the impression that she and I could be twins."

To her surprise, the older woman went pale. Recovering quickly, she gave Sarah a cold smile. "There is a superficial resemblance."

"I understand it's more than that," Sarah retorted.

"Aren't you the little opportunist," Deidre drawled. "Tell me, did you decide to go along with his misidentification before or after you saw the Walker estate?"

Unprepared for the strength of Deidre's animosity, Sarah was still gasping at the full frontal assault when a discreet knock sounded on the door.

"Come in, Juanita," Deidre called.

The maid wheeled in a cart bearing a silver tea service and a plate of thinly sliced fruit. "Would you like me to serve?" she asked.

"I'll take care of it," Deidre replied impatiently. "And see that we aren't disturbed unless Mr. Walker needs me."

To Sarah's surprise, Deidre poured the tea as calmly as if theirs was a friendly meeting and handed Sarah a cup. "Help yourself to some papaya," she invited. "The quality is exceptional."

Sarah would have liked nothing better than to dash the tea in this woman's face and then to leave with her pride intact, but pride wouldn't give her the answers she needed. She set the cup and saucer back down on the tray, ignoring the fruit, and leaned forward in her chair.

"Are you my mother?" she asked bluntly.

Deidre had been about to take a sip of her tea. Her hand shook visibly, nearly spilling the pale amber liquid, and then she, too, set down her cup. The delicate porcelain hit the tray with a bang.

"Where on earth would you get an insane idea like that?" Deidre's expression bordered on loathing. If she had given birth to Sarah and then abandoned her for some unfathomable reason, she might not harbor any maternal feelings, but what kind of mother could hate a child born of her own body?

Suddenly Sarah hoped with all her heart that she didn't share a single gene with this ice queen. Even expensive cosmetics couldn't hide the hardness beneath the sophisticated veneer nor the signs of bitterness that dulled her looks.

"Apparently I look enough like your daughter to fool both Ryan and her grandfather," Sarah couldn't resist pointing out. "Since I happen to be adopted and I don't know the identities of my birth parents, my question isn't entirely ludicrous."

Deidre sat back in her chair, a humorless smile flickering across her face. "I assure you that I am not your mother, nor is my daughter related to you in any way. Apparently your resemblance to her is merely one of those inexplicable coincidences."

She stared at Sarah, unblinking, until Sarah finally looked away, disappointed. If she had been Jessica's twin, unlikely as the idea was, perhaps by marrying her Ryan might not forfeit everything he'd hoped to gain. Now she was back to the very real probability that she would lose him as soon as he found out the truth.

"You must remember that Ryan has never actually met Jessica face-to-face," Deidre continued. "And Stuart's eyesight isn't what it used to be." She rose from the chair and smoothed down her skirt with hands that showed her age despite their carefully manicured nails. A bracelet of heavy gold links adorned her wrist and a large diamond winked on her finger. "Your coloring and general appearance do resemble Jessica's, but you're hardly identical." Her smile was infuriatingly smug. "If you're looking for a pedigree, you've come to the wrong place."

"None of this was my idea," Sarah protested. "I didn't seek you out."

Deidre ignored her comment. "Now you'll have to come back downstairs with me," she said. "After I reveal your little deception to Ryan, a car will take you to the bus station. Where is it that you live?"

"Bellville," Sarah replied as she got to her feet, knowing it would be futile to protest her innocence. She *had* deceived Ryan.

She wished she could meet Jessica, but she knew without asking that Deidre would never allow it. Desperately trying to think what to do next, Sarah let her gaze wander around the lovely bedroom. On one dresser was a grouping of photographs in silver frames.

"What are you doing?" Deidre demanded as Sarah went over for a closer look. "Leave my daughter's things alone."

Sarah picked up a picture of Jessica standing with an attractive young man in a tux. Reaction shivered through Sarah as she studied the other girl's face.

She might as well have been staring at a picture of herself.

There was also a framed snapshot of Jessica and another girl that had obviously been taken on some tropical beach. Wearing straw hats, halter tops and brightly colored sarongs, they mugged for the camera.

Jessica didn't look at all like the stuck-up heiress Sarah had assumed her to be. Her hair was long and wavy, like Sarah's would be if she grew it out past her shoulders, her smile friendly and unpretentious as she stood with her arm draped across her friend's shoulders.

A sharp pain stabbed Sarah like a knife as she imagined her in Ryan's arms as he gazed at her with the same desire Sarah had seen blazing in his eyes. Were she and Jessica interchangeable to him? Would kissing one feel the same as kissing the other?

Sarah glanced at Deidre, who stood frozen in the middle of the room. "All right," Deidre snapped. "I'll admit the resemblance is uncanny, but I would certainly know if you were my daughter, now wouldn't I? Jessica is an only child. Please leave her pictures alone. We're going downstairs."

More confused than ever, Sarah followed Deidre out of the room. When they reached the landing, Ryan was coming up the staircase.

"There you are," he exclaimed when he lifted his head and saw them. He smiled at Sarah. "Stuart is still resting and I got lonesome, so I decided to find you. Did you two have a good visit?"

Before Sarah could think of a tactful reply, Deidre elbowed her aside. When Ryan reached the landing, she placed a detaining hand on his arm. "Come back downstairs with us. There's something you need to know."

He looked from her to Sarah and back again. "Is it Stuart?" he asked.

Deidre merely shook her head and led the way back down the stairs.

"Are you all right?" Ryan asked Sarah softly as he brushed her cheek with his fingers.

She didn't think she could look at him without crying, so she merely shrugged, eyes downcast. "I'm okay."

"Don't worry," he murmured, giving her shoulder a reassuring squeeze. "She may be annoyed with you for leaving the way you did, but I'm sure she'll get over it when we announce our good news."

He took her hand and she clung to him, unwilling to spoil the moment by telling him just how wrong his cheerful assumption really was.

When Jessica didn't respond to Ryan's attempt to reassure her, he followed Deidre back down to the formal room he'd just vacated. A different maid approached, but Deidre waved her away.

Before she left, the maid glanced at Jessica with a startled expression. Apparently news of the prodigal daughter's return had not yet spread among the staff.

"I'd like to talk to Ryan by myself," Jessica told Deidre, hesitating in the entrance to the sunroom. Her cheeks were pale as she turned to face Ryan. Tension radiated from her, stirring a profound sense of foreboding within him. "I have a right to tell him."

"You have no rights here," Deidre replied, startling Ryan as much by her tone as her comment. He had thought she'd be happier to have her daughter back.

"Tell me what?" he demanded.

"This isn't Jessica," Deidre said bluntly. "Frankly, I'm not sure *who* she is."

"What?" Stunned, Ryan could only stare from his

fiancée to the grim-faced woman and back again. Had he heard right? "Jessica? What kind of game is this?"

Sadly, she shook her head. "I'm Sarah, remember? Sarah Daniels from Bellville. I tried to tell you on our way to the cabin, but you didn't believe me." Her blue eyes glittered with tears and her mouth trembled.

Why was she doing this to him?

Past the sudden roaring in his ears, Ryan heard her words and tried to make sense of them. The woman he'd held in his arms *wasn't* Jessica? He shook his head in denial, but part of him knew, from the expressions of the two women facing him—one remorseful and one oddly triumphant—that what he was hearing was true.

"How could this have happened?" he muttered to no one in particular.

"Obviously a good part of the blame lies with Miss Daniels," Deidre commented. "If she had truly wanted to convince you, she could have. She must have realized she was onto a good thing."

Ryan shook his head, trying to get past the waves of confusion and think clearly. None of this made any sense. Even Stuart had identified the engagement photo as Jessica. Ryan was tempted to grab the lifeline Deidre had tossed him and to blame Sarah. His mind stuttered over the unfamiliar name. But she had tried to tell him the truth in the beginning. Why then, had she stopped?

"I can imagine that you're shocked," Deidre exclaimed with a brittle laugh. "Our little fortune hunter does resemble Jessica to a certain extent, but of course she couldn't fool me.''

''She's a dead ringer,'' he contradicted, ''and she's no fortune hunter. She was honest with me, but I wouldn't believe her.'' He glanced at Sarah, trying to read her expression. Lord, what a mess. He'd never do anything impulsive again!

''We'll sort it out after she leaves,'' Deidre said briskly. ''And then we'll renew our search for my daughter. I certainly don't think there's any reason to concern Stuart with any of this. Meanwhile, I'll have someone bring the car around.'' She headed for the door.

Ryan spoke before she could open it. ''Why didn't you say something when we first got here instead of pretending she was Jessica?''

Deidre turned slowly. ''I miss my daughter terribly,'' she replied. ''You told me you were bringing her home with you. When you arrived, I was stunned to see not Jessica but *her*.'' She gestured toward Sarah. ''Naturally it took me a few moments to recover.''

It was difficult for Ryan to imagine her in less than total control, but he supposed her shock was understandable under the circumstances. ''I want a few moments of privacy with Sarah,'' he said.

''I don't think that's necessary—'' Deidre protested.

''But I do,'' he replied firmly, having no intentions of being outmaneuvered before he got some answers.

Deidre's color rose as she hesitated with her hand

on the knob. Why didn't she want him to talk to Sarah alone? Was Deidre hiding something? But what?

"Very well, then." Abruptly she left, shutting the door behind her.

As soon as she was gone, Sarah came over to Ryan. She lifted her hand as though she was going to touch him, but then she let it drop back to her side.

"I love you," she said quietly. "I hope you believe that."

The bold words came as a dash of cold water. It was Jessica he had thought was in love with him, not this woman he didn't know. But *this woman* was the one who had captivated him, the one who had given him her virginity. Jessica, he must remember, was still the stranger he'd only seen across a crowd of party-goers.

Ryan didn't know what to think, and he sure as hell had no idea what he was feeling except confusion. He raked his hand through his hair as he studied Sarah's face and tried not to remember what it felt like to be buried inside her.

Dammit, feelings weren't supposed to enter into this. He knew better. Marrying Jessica was supposed to be a business decision, pure and simple. Except that *nothing* about this situation was simple any more.

"I don't want you leaving here until we've sorted this out," he surprised himself by telling her.

"What do you mean?" she asked with a quaver in her voice. "Are you saying you still don't believe who I am?"

He shook his head impatiently. "Of course I believe you.'' He grabbed her shoulders and searched her face. ''Is there anything, *anything,* you know about your background that you haven't told me?''

''Like what?'' she asked, frowning.

''I don't know.'' He let her go. ''You said you were adopted. Is there a possibility that you could be related to the Walkers in some way?''

''All I know is what I was told by the people who raised me, that I had been abandoned at the Bellville hospital as an infant,'' she replied. ''No clues to my identity were ever found. That's it in a nutshell.''

''Okay,'' Ryan muttered, disappointed. ''I've got a feeling that Deidre knows more than she's saying, and I want to talk to Stuart before you go.''

Sarah's shoulders slumped and her gaze slid away from his. ''Oh.'' Her voice had lost its vibrancy. What did she want from him, anyway?

He was tempted to take her in his arms and tell her not to worry, but something held him back. ''Don't you want to know for sure whether you have a connection to Jessica?'' he demanded instead.

''Of course I do, but Deidre insisted there is no connection,'' Sarah replied. ''Why would she lie?''

''Hell, I don't know, but I intend to find out,'' Ryan said grimly. ''Meanwhile, promise me that you won't leave.''

''How can I stay? She's made it very clear I'm not welcome here.'' She was pale except for the smudges under her eyes, reminding him that he wasn't the only one upset by the bizarre situation.

"Leave Deidre to me," he said. "Do I have your promise?"

Sarah moistened her lips with her tongue and a surge of pure lust shot through him. How could he still want her when he didn't even know her?

"I'm not going to promise," she said, "but I'll do my best to tell you first if I do leave."

"Okay." Ryan wasn't happy with her answer, but he didn't figure on getting anywhere by pressing her and he wasn't ready to analyze why he was so determined to keep her here. "Let's go find Deidre and see where she wants to put you."

"I think I can answer that one," Sarah muttered, wishing Ryan would take her into his arms and tell her that everything was going to be okay. He'd barely reacted to her declaration of love.

When they opened the door, she wasn't surprised to find Deidre hovering outside. Sarah watched her expression change as Ryan explained that he didn't want Sarah to leave just yet.

Deidre shook her head before he was finished talking. "No," she interrupted, holding up both hands as though she were warding off a blow. "That's impossible."

"Then she can stay at my place or I'll put her up at the local hotel," Ryan said, folding his arms across his chest.

Deidre slanted a glance at Sarah that was bristling with resentment. "If she stays here, there's no reason for Stuart to know," she told Ryan. "Not until he's stronger."

"I don't like the idea of keeping it from him," Ryan argued.

"Those are my terms," Deidre said stubbornly. "I won't allow his health to be jeopardized by this situation."

Ryan, too, glanced at Sarah, who was wondering if she had made a mistake in agreeing to stay where she was so clearly unwelcome. No, there was too much at stake for her to allow Deidre to run her off now.

"What about your staff?" Ryan asked. "Sarah can't hide in her room. Won't someone mention her presence to Stuart?"

"Not if they value their jobs."

"What do you think?" he asked Sarah, who was beginning to resent being discussed as though she wasn't present.

"Will you be staying here, too?" She needed him with her. Even though his reaction to the truth hadn't been all that she'd hoped, at least he hadn't turned his back on her totally. Not yet. She'd known from the beginning what his motives were, so she could hardly fault him now for his reluctance to abandon them.

"I'll be at my condo, but it's not far away," he said.

She wished he would take her with him, but she wasn't about to suggest it in front of the older woman and risk his rejection. If he had wanted her there, he would have invited her.

* * *

Deidre was still shaking with frustration when she shut the door to her private rooms behind her, sat down at her antique rolltop desk and retrieved a small book of phone numbers from a locked drawer. Ryan had left to take care of some pressing business, promising to return in a couple of hours, and the creature he'd brought with him was safely stashed in one of the guest rooms in another wing. She had strict orders to stay put until either Ryan returned or Deidre came to fetch her, which she was in no hurry to do. Let the girl stew for a while.

Deidre still resented the high-handed way Ryan had manipulated her into allowing Sarah to stay at the mansion, but she couldn't risk him alerting Stuart to the situation until Deidre had figured out how much about it to admit.

It had been over two decades since she'd laid eyes on Sarah, and she'd hoped at the time never to see her again. Now everything Deidre had worked so hard for was in danger of slipping through her fingers.

If Stuart ever found out what she had done...

If only her plan to strengthen her position here by marrying Jessica to Stuart's protégé had worked out! It still might, if she could persuade Ryan to cooperate, but she'd seen how he looked at Sarah. Getting him to let her go might not be as easy as Deidre had first thought.

One thing was for certain; she would never go back to the pathetic middle-class existence she'd had before she'd been lucky enough to catch the eye of her late husband. Maybe she hadn't been able to produce an heir in the five years they were married before his untimely death, but she'd used every bit of cunning she possessed to secure her place as his widow, rejecting many opportunities to remarry through the years. She wasn't about to chance losing her exalted position in local society at this point in her life.

Not after she'd been fortunate enough to find Larissa Summers, a dancer Stuart had managed to impregnate before his demise. It hadn't been easy for Deidre to persuade Larissa to give up one of the twins she was carrying, but everyone had their price. After Larissa failed to track down Lawrence, who'd had the foresight to give her a false name, she'd finally agreed to allow Deidre, using an alias herself, to adopt one of her babies.

How fortunate for Deidre that Larissa had been too sedated to realize she'd given birth not to twins, but to three identical baby girls. Deidre had paid the midwife handsomely to keep her mouth shut and taken two of the babies with her. Twice the generous trust funds she planned on getting from Stuart were better than one. It hadn't been Deidre's fault that one of the babies got sick and she'd had to abandon it. At least she had been kind enough to leave the infant at a hospital where it would receive proper care.

She'd brought the healthy baby back to Willow Springs and presented the child to Stuart. After a blood test indicated that Jessica could indeed be his grandchild, he'd been more than willing to provide generously for her and for Deidre.

At the time he hadn't wanted to know any of the

lurid details and Deidre hadn't told him. Over the years, she had come to love Jessica dearly, and she'd devoted her life to raising the child with every advantage that Deidre herself had gone without. It was only when Stuart began talking about a match between Jessica and Ryan that Deidre had seen a golden opportunity to make sure that Stuart was never able to turn her out.

Or so she'd thought.

If he ever found out after all this time that Lawrence had left him two more granddaughters, Jessica's sisters, and that Deidre had kept the information from him, he would never forgive her. No matter what the cost, Deidre had to make sure that neither he nor Ryan ever tracked down Larissa Summers.

Hands shaking, Deidre opened the small book and found the number she'd been looking for. After two calls, she finally connected with a man whose voice sent shivers down her spine. She gave him all the information she had on Larissa and told him what she wanted done.

The man she'd contacted came very well recommended. Once he sighted his target, the loose end named Larissa need never concern Deidre again.

Sarah had tried to nap in the guest room she'd been assigned earlier, but sleep wouldn't come. Finally she gave up. After she'd repaired her makeup and brushed her hair, grateful for the toiletries she'd insisted on buying earlier, she stood at the window overlooking the stables and hoped that Quincy's visit to the estate was going better than hers. She would have liked to walk down there and visit the dog, but there was no point in antagonizing Deidre any more than Sarah's mere presence already did.

Was Ryan right? Did Jessica's mother know more than she was admitting to? Before he'd left, promising to return as soon as possible, he'd mentioned to her the possibility of hiring an investigator if Deidre wasn't forthcoming. That and his expression, a mixture of longing and regret, were the only encouraging signs Sarah had been able to cling to since he'd gone.

There were several books and magazines in the room, but none of them held her interest. She hadn't eaten since lunch and her stomach felt hollow. Finally, even though she had agreed to wait until Deidre came for her, she decided to look for one of the maids and see if she could get something to eat.

Sarah made her way back to the main staircase and down to the first floor without running into another soul. She would have liked to examine more closely the rooms she passed, each one filled with beautiful furnishings and objets d'art, but she didn't want to confront Deidre.

Eventually she found a narrower hallway that branched off the main corridor. She must be getting closer to the kitchen. Breathing a sigh of relief, she passed a set of open double doors leading to what must be the library. Overhead lights illuminated floor to ceiling bookcases and a jewel-toned Persian carpet covered the floor. Unable to resist, she peeked inside.

Flanking a marble fireplace were two wing back

chairs. Seated in one next to a Tiffany lamp was an older man with silver hair and an aristocratic profile, a book open on his lap. He had to be Jessica's grandfather, Stuart.

Both Ryan and Deidre would be furious with Sarah for upsetting him in any way. Holding her breath, she started to back away as silently as possible when he glanced up and saw her.

"Jessica!" he exclaimed, closing the book and getting to his feet with a welcoming smile on his lined face. "When did you get back?"

Dismayed, Sarah shrank away, but he advanced on her with his arms outstretched. "Come and say hello."

Glancing behind her, Sarah saw no assistance in sight. Reluctantly she stepped from the dimly lit hallway into the brighter light of the library. When she did, Stuart's smile faded, to be replaced by an expression of puzzlement.

"My God," he breathed, his blue eyes wide. "You aren't Jessica. Who *are* you?"

Chapter Eleven

"I said, who are you?" Stuart repeated impatiently, staring at her over the tops of his reading glasses. "Is this some kind of trick?"

"I—I'm sorry," Sarah stammered. "I was looking for the kitchen, but I wasn't supposed to bother you." She knew there was no way he was going to allow her to leave without some explanation.

"You look just like my granddaughter," he said. Despite his deeply lined face, it was easy to see he had once been a handsome man and still maintained an air of authority that would command attention. In addition, he was someone Ryan held in the highest regard, enough so to marry a woman he didn't love and barely knew.

"I'm Stuart Walker," he added unnecessarily. "Why don't you come in and sit down."

With a guilty glance over her shoulder, Sarah ventured into the room and perched on the edge of a chair while he sat down opposite her and set his glasses on a marble-topped side table.

"What's your name?" he asked.

"I'm Sarah Daniels."

For a long moment his gaze searched her face, his blue eyes bright and intelligent beneath thick brows. She suspected the cardigan sweater he wore with an open-necked shirt was more casual than was his habit. It was easy to imagine him wearing a dark suit with a white shirt and conservative silk tie, even when he wasn't working.

"Unbelievable," he murmured.

"Do I really look like Jessica?" she asked timidly.

"You could be her twin." His complexion had a gray tinge, reminding her that he wasn't entirely well.

"Are you feeling all right?" she asked, concerned. "Should I call someone?" She started to rise, but he gestured for her to stay put.

"I'm stronger than I look. My daughter-in-law tends to exaggerate." His gaze narrowed. "I take it that you've met Deidre?"

Sarah nodded, unsure what to say or how much to tell him. How she wished she had remained in the guest room until Ryan returned, but if she had, she might not have met this man who might very well be her own grandfather.

He crossed one leg over the other, hitching up the

dark fabric of his slacks, and folded his hands on his knee. A heavy college ring with a deep red stone looked too big for one bony finger.

"Tell me about yourself and how you happen to be here," he suggested. "Start from the beginning, and don't leave anything out."

While Sarah talked, his expression remained impassive. He didn't interrupt until she got to the part about Ryan kidnapping her from her wedding.

"I'm sorry that happened." Stuart sounded genuinely regretful. "It must have been your newspaper photo I identified as Jessica's. Have you called your young man to let him know you're all right?"

"Not exactly. I talked to his sister," Sarah admitted, "but she's pretty upset with me." Briefly she explained about the letter she'd written and must have dropped when she fainted.

"The telephones here are at your disposal," Stuart replied. "I'm sure he'll understand when you explain everything."

Sarah sent a horrified glance to the phone sitting on an antique writing table. She had no idea what she was going to say to Dan.

Stuart must have intercepted her look. "I didn't mean for you to call from here," he exclaimed, leaning forward to pat her hand. His felt warm and dry, almost papery. "I'm sure you'll want some privacy when you speak to him. Lord knows there are enough rooms in this mausoleum for you to find one that's unoccupied, and they all have telephones."

"Thank you," Sarah responded, absently pleating the fabric of her skirt with her fingers.

When was Ryan coming back? She missed him terribly, although the old anniversary clock on the mantle indicated that he'd only been gone a little over two hours.

"Meanwhile," Stuart continued, "I intend getting to the bottom of this mystery surrounding your background."

Before she could ask what he planned to do about it, he pressed a button on the table next to the Tiffany lamp. Within moments one of the maids Sarah had noticed earlier appeared in the doorway.

"Tell Deidre I want to see her right away," Stuart said. Despite his kindly air toward Sarah, it was easy to see he was used to having his orders obeyed without question. The maid nodded and hurried off to do his bidding. Sarah nearly felt sorry for Deidre until she reminded herself that the other woman might very well hold the key to Sarah's real identity.

When Deidre walked into the library and saw Sarah with Stuart, she stopped dead in her tracks. Her eyes widened and a flash of what looked like fear crossed her face before she regained control of her expression. She didn't speak as her gaze darted back and forth as though she were trying to assess the situation.

"Sit down," Stuart snapped, gesturing abruptly to a side chair by the window.

Cheeks flushing unbecomingly, Deidre dropped into the chair with a jerky movement that lacked her usual poise. Her chin was high, her expression resentful. Her hand revealed her turmoil, trembling when she reached up to toy with one tiny gold earring.

"I won't be summoned like a schoolgirl," she said hotly. "If you need something—"

"What I *need* is an explanation," Stuart cut in ruthlessly. "What the *hell* is going on here?"

"I don't know what you mean." Deidre's eyes narrowed, but her voice was surprisingly calm, considering that she reminded Sarah of someone who'd been cornered. What was she hiding?

The flat of Stuart's hand slapped the tabletop with a loud crack, making both women jump.

"Look at her!" he exclaimed, pointing to Sarah. "It's as plain as her face that she's related to our darling girl. You're the one who adopted Jessica—"

Sarah's mouth dropped open. Ryan hadn't mentioned that! Perhaps he didn't know. Then she realized that, no matter what, there was no chance that Deidre was her biological mother. In the midst of her tumultuous feelings was a small island of relief.

"Sarah is adopted, too," Stuart continued.

"It's only a coincidence," Deidre replied. "It doesn't mean anything. Thousands of babies—"

"Thousands of babies aren't clones of each other," Stuart cut in with a sneer. "I want the truth." He leaned forward and shook his finger at her. "If you won't tell me right now everything you know about this, I'll have someone else dig it out."

"Think of the publicity, if the press gets wind of it," Deidre cried.

"The hell with the press. If I find out you've been keeping something from me that I should know, I'll toss you out of here on your well-maintained derriere. And won't the press love that!"

His voice had grown in volume as he talked. Sarah felt like an intruder in a very private family argument, but she had a stake in this, too, and she desperately wanted to know the truth.

Deidre was staring at Stuart, her eyes brimming with tears that, amazingly, didn't fall and spoil her mascara. Sarah watched, fascinated, as she rose on legs that seemed to wobble, her full lower lip trembling, and approached her father-in-law with one hand outstretched in supplication.

"Stuart," she began with a quaver in her voice.

"What's going on here?" Ryan demanded from the doorway.

At the sight of him, Sarah had to restrain herself from leaping up and running straight into his arms. Only the realization that they might not open for her kept her in her chair.

To Sarah's surprise and Stuart's obvious disgust, Deidre *did* run to Ryan, throwing her arms around his neck and bursting into noisy sobs as she buried her face in his chest. His puzzled gaze locked on Sarah as he reached up and peeled Deidre's arms away.

"Pull up a chair. You might as well join us," Stuart invited in a dry voice.

Ryan gave him a crooked grin that didn't hide his genuine affection for the older man. "How are you feeling?'' he asked. ''I thought you were at death's door.''

''I never told you that!'' Deidre exclaimed as Stuart uttered a word that startled Sarah with its bluntness.

''Everyone's so damned concerned for my health,'' he growled. ''Anyone would think you've all been reading my will.''

''Actually we ran off copies and sold them to the tabloids for six bits apiece.'' Ryan gave Sarah a sly wink as he grabbed a straight-back chair in one hand and set it down next to where she was seated.

Stuart turned a chuckle into a cough. ''You sold them too cheap.'' His expression sobered again. ''Sarah told me what happened between you.''

Ryan stared at her, wide-eyed. ''You did?''

''Yes, I told him you kidnapped me from my own wedding,'' she agreed quickly, hoping he would understand that she hadn't told Stuart *everything*.

Understanding dawned in his eyes. ''I see.''

''When you arrived, we were just getting to the part concerning Sarah's relationship to Jessica,'' Stuart continued, steepling his fingers under his chin. ''I believe Deidre was about to explain it all to us.''

Deidre sat back down and took the handkerchief that Stuart shoved at her. Dabbing at her eyes, she managed a watery smile.

''I've been thinking about the coincidence of both girls being adopted,'' she said softly, ''and I've come to the conclusion that the only possible explanation is that the woman who entrusted Jessica to my care must have given birth to twins and for some nefarious reason of her own not told me about the other baby.''

"Jessica was adopted, too?" Ryan asked.

"My son had his faults," Stuart said, frowning. "After he was killed, it came to Deidre's attention that a woman he'd been involved with was going to have his child." He glanced at her and she nodded in agreement. "Since Deidre hadn't been able to provide Lawrence with a baby, she contacted the woman and persuaded her to allow Deidre to adopt Jessica."

"I knew how much Stuart wanted an heir," Deidre added, "and Jessica is my daughter in every way but one."

"That doesn't explain the biological mother's possible motive for keeping it a secret if she'd given birth to twins," Ryan pointed out. "I'm assuming you helped her out a little with her expenses."

Deidre hesitated before nodding. "I had no choice."

"Wouldn't she have assumed you'd pay double for two babies?"

Deidre leaped to her feet. "How should I know what she thought? Maybe she figured on getting more for the second baby if she waited awhile. Maybe something happened to her and someone else left the other baby at that hospital."

She looked at Sarah, fresh tears welling in her eyes. "All I know is that as soon as I find my own precious Jessica—" Her voice broke and she bowed her head for a moment. Swallowing, she cleared her throat and continued on. "I will do whatever I can to help clear up this mystery," she vowed.

"Sarah, are you all right?" Ryan asked, breaking into her thoughts.

She stared at him, blinking a couple of times in an effort to focus on her immediate surroundings. "I might be a twin," she mumbled as the possibility sank in. "Do you know what that means? I could have a sister!"

Ryan patted her hand. "I think it's a very real possibility."

She pressed her fingers to her mouth to keep it from trembling. Because of Ryan and the love Sarah had for him, her feelings about the other girl were certainly mixed, but she was still avidly curious.

"Maybe when Jessica comes back, you could let me know," she said to Stuart. "I'd like to meet her."

Stuart was staring intently. "I'll make a few calls in the morning, but I don't have any doubt who you are. Why don't you stay here for the time being? We can get to know each other and, if Jessica should come home on her own, you'll be here to meet her."

"Well, I do have some vacation time left," Sarah said. She'd taken two weeks off from the bank for her honeymoon and to move her things into Dan's apartment.

"Fine." Stuart took her hands in his and bent down to give her a kiss on the cheek. "Welcome to the family," he said, voice husky.

Sarah was overwhelmed by his acceptance. "Thank you," she murmured.

He sat back down and cleared his throat. "We have the pool, the tennis courts and a fine stable. Perhaps Ryan would consent to keep you company when he's not running his empire."

Sarah glanced at him from beneath her lashes, mortified that he might feel obligated to entertain her. His mouth had tightened at Stuart's blatant suggestion. Ryan's gaze met hers and he tipped his head.

"I'm sure we can think of something to do."

What on earth did he mean by that?

A knock on the closed library door broke the awkward silence that followed his comment.

"What is it?" Stuart called out.

An older man stuck his head through the doorway. "Would you like dinner at the usual time?" he asked, speaking with an English accent.

Stuart glanced at Ryan. "Won't you stay for dinner? There are a few things I want to discuss with you afterwards."

Sarah dreaded the idea of facing Deidre across the table, but it would be infinitely worse without Ryan here. She held her breath until he said, "Sure, why not?"

"There will be four of us," Stuart told the man waiting at the door.

"Very good, sir," he replied and then he disappeared.

Sarah had to smother a nervous giggle. She couldn't imagine getting used to all these servants running around.

Ryan got to his feet and extended his hand to her.

"Sarah, you must be exhausted by all this. May I walk you back to your room?"

She grabbed his outstretched hand as though it were a lifeline and got up to stand beside him. "Thank you. I don't think I could have found my way back on my own."

Deidre was the only one who didn't laugh at her admission.

Stuart rose, a smile softening his stern features. "You've got time to rest before dinner," he said. "We'll see you then."

Sarah wasn't sure what to say. Was he implying that she looked tired? The last half hour had certainly been an emotional drain. She still had to sort out her feelings. Settling for a nod and a smile, she allowed Ryan to lead her from the room.

Dinner was an awkward affair. Ryan had eaten here a couple of times before, but Jessica had been away on a trip or out for the evening. How much simpler his life would be now if his path had actually crossed hers, but his relationship with Stuart, although close, had been a professional one until very recently. Although Ryan had met Deidre on several occasions, they didn't normally socialize with the same people.

He glanced at Sarah, who was making a pretense of eating the excellent roast chicken, and wondered what she was thinking. When he had walked her back to the guest room after the very enlightening meeting earlier, he'd wanted to reassure her. Instead he'd succumbed to temptation and hauled her into his arms.

He wondered now if she had sensed the desperation behind his kiss before she melted against him.

Part of him had wanted to kick the door shut behind them and rediscover the magic they had shared back at the cabin. The part that was capable of rational thought had restrained him. He knew she wanted him to tell her he loved her, but the words stuck in his throat. He recalled the hurt in her eyes when he'd finally mumbled an excuse and left her standing alone in the guest room doorway.

"Why don't you show Sarah the stables in the morning," Stuart suggested, snapping Ryan out of his thoughts. Stuart turned to her, seated on his left at the rectangular dining room table. She was still wearing the same dress Ryan had bought for her earlier. "Do you ride, my dear?"

Sarah shook her head. "I'd love to see the horses, though." She glanced at Ryan. "And check on Quincy."

"Who's Quincy?" Stuart asked.

"He's a stray dog we found in the woods near the cabin," Ryan explained. "I gave him to Ben when we arrived and asked him to turn Quincy over to Charlie for safekeeping."

"Was the dog lost, do you think?" Stuart asked.

Ryan shook his head. "I'm pretty sure someone dumped him. The local deputy up there is going to see if he's been reported missing and get back to me."

Stuart nodded and the conversation died again. Finally, after their plates were cleared and a dessert course was served that no one touched, Stuart laid his napkin on the table and slid back his chair.

"Ryan, come with me to the study," he said. "I've got a fine old brandy there I'd like you to sample."

Feeling like a schoolboy who'd been summoned to the principal's office, Ryan nodded and got to his feet.

"Ladies, if you'll excuse us," Stuart said. "Deidre, make sure Sarah has whatever she needs. Jessica's closets are full to overflowing and she'll never miss a few items."

Resentment flashed across Deidre's face. "You want me to lend her *Jessica's* clothes?"

Stuart's expression hardened. "Or yours," he drawled. "Take your pick."

Before she could reply, Sarah spoke up. "I don't need anything, thank you." She glanced at Ryan. "We did a little shopping on the way here, so I'm fine."

"If you change your mind, be sure to let Deidre know," Stuart told her firmly. After she had repeated her thanks, he led Ryan from the dining room without glancing at his daughter-in-law again.

Ryan was inclined to stick around and make sure Deidre wasn't going to light into Sarah the moment he and Stuart were out of earshot, but Stuart began talking about an acquaintance who was looking for a white knight to bail his company out of a difficult situation. At the door to Stuart's study, Ryan was finally able to glance back in time to see Deidre walking alone in the other direction.

Leaving the door open, Stuart crossed to the built-in bar and poured two brandies. Handing one to Ryan, he sat down in a leather chair and waited for Ryan to join him.

"I like your Sarah," he said bluntly.

Ryan swirled the dark liquid in the balloon glass and inhaled the aroma that wafted upward. If Stuart wanted to be blunt, Ryan would accommodate him.

"Your intention was that I marry Jessica," he reminded his mentor.

Stuart set down his glass with a chuckle. "That's true. You were willing to do that and I appreciate it more than I can say. But my reasons for wanting that union would also apply to Sarah."

"If she's really your granddaughter," Ryan reminded him, ignoring the surge of excitement that rose inside him in response to Stuart's statement. "You have no proof of that yet."

Stuart wave his hand in a dismissive gesture. "I have all the proof I need that she's Jessica's twin and Lawrence's daughter," he replied, leaning forward. "Am I right in assuming the reason you were bringing her back was because the two of you had reached an agreement of a personal nature?"

Ryan nodded, his throat tightening. "She accepted my proposal."

He could hardly bear to recall the exhilaration that had flowed through him when she finally said yes. It had nothing to do with satisfying Stuart and everything to do with obtaining what Ryan wanted for himself. Remembering the way she'd come into his arms and the love on her face before they'd sealed their bargain with a kiss was too damned painful to contemplate.

"Well," Stuart said, rubbing his hands together, "that's fine. My intention was to ensure the future of my company once I'm too senile to run it, and to guarantee the continuing financial security of my descendants. Taking into consideration what we learned today, whichever one of my granddaughters you choose to marry would certainly serve my purpose."

"Let me get this absolutely clear," Ryan replied, struggling to keep his voice even. "Are you telling me that whether it's Jessica or Sarah that I marry, you and I will proceed with the business partnership we discussed before?"

"That's right," Stuart said with an emphatic nod. "One or the other, it makes no difference to me."

Outside the study, Sarah sagged against the wall as bile rose in her throat. She hadn't intended to eavesdrop, but she'd been walking by and heard her name mentioned. How she wished now that she'd kept going with her hands clamped over her ears.

Neither Stuart nor Ryan cared which twin he married. In their eyes, in his arms, in his bed, Jessica and Sarah were interchangeable.

Sarah drew in a shaky breath as the truth sank in, wounding her like a thousand tiny knives. Once Ryan had found out she wasn't the heiress he believed her to be, he'd backed off. Now that she had the Walker stamp of approval and Ryan didn't stand to lose what he really wanted—power and money—it appeared she was back in the running. How much more convenient for Ryan than to start over with Jessica.

Wasn't Sarah lucky?

They were still talking, but she couldn't make out the words past the roaring in her ears. Heart breaking at his callousness, hand pressed to her mouth to stifle her sobs, she turned and hurried blindly down the hall.

Back in the library, Ryan struggled to keep from grabbing Stuart and hugging him for letting him off the hook.

"I'm glad to hear you say that it doesn't matter to you which sister I marry," he said instead, "because the truth is that it matters a hell of a lot to me. I was trying to figure out how to break the news to you I can't marry Jessica after all. I guess I knew that the moment I found out that Jessica wasn't the one I'd proposed to."

"I thought there was something going on between you and Sarah," Stuart remarked with a satisfied smile. "I guess congratulations are in order."

"Not yet," Ryan replied with a rueful shake of his head. "I think there's some fence mending I need to do first." He started to rise, but Stuart waved him back down.

"Before you leave, we need to go over our offer to bail out that security firm in Reno," he reminded Ryan. "I want to fax it first thing in the morning."

Ryan struggled to curb his impatience, but at least he knew where to find Sarah the moment he was finished here.

* * *

"What's wrong with you?" Deidre asked when she saw Sarah rushing toward her with distress written all over her face. It was difficult for Deidre to even look at the girl when she had no idea where Jessica was or even if she was all right. It sickened her to think of Sarah cooped up at the cabin with Ryan when it was Jessica that Deidre had planned for him to marry.

Sarah hesitated, glancing over her shoulder as though she was being followed by a bogeyman. "I want to go back to Bellville," she said, startling Deidre. "I don't want Ryan to know I'm leaving. Will you help me?"

Deidre couldn't believe her luck. Trouble between Ryan and Sarah could mean another opportunity for him and Jessica. Besides, with Sarah out of the picture, Stuart's search for Larissa Summers might be delayed until Deidre's own man had a chance to locate her.

"Of course I'll help you," she told Sarah in as soothing a voice as she could manage. Taking the girl's arm, Deidre steered her away from the study, her mind working quickly. "Come with me while I arrange for someone to drive you back to Bellville where you belong."

Chapter Twelve

What a relief to wake up in her own bed, Sarah thought as she stretched and opened her eyes the next morning. It had been very late when she got back to Bellville and she'd been worn out both emotionally and physically. Luckily she kept a spare apartment key hidden in the planter by the front door, so she'd been able to let herself in without disturbing anyone.

She hadn't thought she'd sleep a wink after what she overheard between Ryan and Stuart, but when her head hit the pillow she went out like a light. No matter what happened with Jessica, Sarah would have to get over her feelings for Ryan before he became her brother-in-law. The idea of having an identical twin was still pretty new to her, but already she knew marrying someone who thought they were interchangeable wasn't something she could live with.

She had thought Ryan had begun to love her for herself, but she had heard differently with her own ears. Maybe she'd been wrong and he just wasn't capable of the depth of feelings she needed from the man to whom she gave her heart to.

Before the car had come for her, she had scribbled a note to Ryan that Deidre had promised to deliver. If he really loved her, Sarah Daniels, and not just Walker heiress number two, perhaps he would understand why'd she'd had to leave, and he would come after her. If she didn't hear from him, she would know she'd been right. In his eyes and in his heart, either twin would do.

Determined not to start crying again, Sarah got up and padded to the kitchen in search of coffee. Most of her belongings were sitting around in packing boxes, ready for the big move after the wedding that never took place. Maybe Sarah had felt some kind of premonition, because she'd never gotten around to actually taking anything over to Dan's. She'd been too busy planning for the wedding, and she'd insisted there would be plenty of time to move her after they got back from Vegas, and Dan had agreed.

Dan. She owed him a face-to-face explanation and the poor man had waited long enough. Who knew what his sister had told him after Sarah called her or what he was thinking.

Bellville was a small town. As soon as she showered and dressed, she was going to find him.

* * *

Ryan stared at his computer monitor without seeing what was on the screen. A cup of coffee that had grown cold sat untouched at his elbow. Next to it was the note Deidre had given him the night before.

I guess I didn't need to pretend I was Jessica after all to get what I wanted. Good luck with her.
Sarah Daniels

It was painfully obvious that she no longer had any use for Ryan or what he could give her. He hadn't slept a wink, berating himself for misjudging her so completely. He'd known better than to let emotion cloud his reason, and now he was paying the price.

Sarah had driven by Dan's apartment, but he wasn't there. As much as she dreaded confronting his parents, their house was the next logical place for him to be, unless he'd gone out of town on his own.

Her feelings were mixed when she saw his pickup parked next to his mother's car in the driveway. She had hoped to talk to Dan in private.

Moments later when Sarah rang the bell, Rose answered the door. Her welcoming smile turned to surprise, but at least she didn't slam the door in Sarah's face. Instead she opened it wider.

"Come in, dear. I'm glad to see that you're all right, at least."

"Thank you. I want you to know that I'm sorry for everything that's happened. Is Dan here?" Sarah asked, feeling terribly awkward.

"He's in the kitchen." She led the way through the

neat rambler that was almost as familiar to Sarah as the home where she'd grown up.

"Dan, look who's here," Rose called.

He glanced up from his seat at the table where he'd been reading the newspaper.

"Sarah!" He leaped to his feet, nearly spilling his coffee. "What are you doing here? Where have you been?"

She'd expected him to be angry, and it was plain to see that he was. His face was flushed and his expression was hostile.

"I need to talk to you." She was so sorry that he'd been hurt by everything that had happened, but there was no way she could go back, not even if he still wanted her.

He glanced at his mother, who was already reaching for her purse.

"I have some errands," she announced. "Might as well do them now." She looked at Sarah. "I know you must have had a good reason for what you did," she said, "and I'm not going to judge you."

"Thank you," Sarah whispered, unable to say she was sorry again without starting to cry. "I appreciate your saying that."

Rose walked over to Dan and gave him a hug he didn't return. After she'd told him that she loved him, she left without looking at Sarah again.

After the door closed behind her, Sarah waited for Dan to say something. Finally he gestured to the chair she always used when she came over.

"You might as well sit down." His tone was less

than gracious, and he didn't offer her any coffee, but she couldn't have choked it down anyway.

He sat across from her and folded his hands on the table. "Why didn't you tell me you changed your mind instead of leaving that letter?" he demanded, a muscle jumping in his cheek.

All of a sudden, Sarah realized that she wasn't going to tell him the whole convoluted story of her abduction and how she'd ended up falling for the man responsible. What was the point in going through all that when she and Dan had no possible future together?

"I'm sorry that I hurt you," she told him, holding his gaze even though she would have rather looked away. "I should have done things a lot differently, but I was a coward and I humiliated you." Now the tears did come, but she blinked them back. "I hope someday you can forgive me."

"Where have you been for the last four days?" he asked. "We were all worried about you."

Now she did bow her head. "I know, and I'm sorry. I've been staying at a friend's cabin."

"Who do you know that has a cabin?" he asked.

"It doesn't matter. Did Kelly tell you I called yesterday?"

"Yeah. She's pretty torn up by all this."

"I can understand that." Sarah brushed the tears away from her cheeks and dug in her purse for a tissue.

"Do you want some water?" Dan asked.

She nodded and then she wiped her nose. When he

handed her the glass, she thanked him before she took a sip.

"What did I do wrong?" he asked as he resumed his seat opposite her.

Sarah was just beginning to realize the extent of the hurt she had inflicted on him, not only by what she hadn't been able to control, but also by accepting his proposal in the first place. He was a perfectly nice man, but she just hadn't loved him the way he deserved.

"Listen to me," she exclaimed so sharply that she startled him. "Don't blame yourself for any of this."

"I'm not," he protested.

"I mean it," she continued firmly as if he hadn't spoken. "You're a wonderful man and you'll find someone who appreciates that. I'm only sorry I wasn't able to, and that I didn't realize it in time to spare you so much embarrassment."

He was frowning as he listened to her. "Are you saying you never loved me?" he demanded.

Sarah shook her head, struggling to keep her voice steady. "No, I'm not. You probably don't believe me right now, but I do love you, and your parents and Kelly, too. The fault is with me, not you. I guess I was trying to replace the family I'd lost. I'm sorry," she repeated, pushing back her chair. "I hope that someday you can forgive me."

He didn't say anything as she stood up, just looked at her with an unreadable expression, so she turned around and headed back through the living room.

Dan called her name before she got to the door.

Sarah looked around to see that he'd followed her from the kitchen.

"Take care of yourself," he said gruffly.

Nodding, fresh tears blinding her vision, Sarah opened the door and fled.

After a two-week absence, Sarah had returned to her job at the bank. Facing everyone and dealing with their questions hadn't been easy.

Rose had called and offered to return the wedding gifts, which had all been stored at her house, but Sarah felt it was her job to contact the guests personally and thank them for their understanding. The looks she got and whispered comments were finally getting less frequent, but she was still thinking about starting over somewhere else.

She and Kelly had talked a few times, but the strain was still there between them. Kelly felt betrayed and Sarah didn't blame her. Without the companionship of Dan's family that Sarah had gotten so used to, there wasn't a lot to keep her here in Bellville. She hadn't heard a word from anyone in Willow Springs, but she hoped that Stuart would invite her back to meet Jessica when she came home.

Sarah missed Quincy and she wondered whether the deputy had found his owner, if he was still at the Walkers' stable or if Ryan had taken him in. The man needed something more than tropical fish to keep him company.

She missed Ryan most of all. She'd clung to the faint hope that by now he might have thought about

what she'd tried to tell him in her note and would
have gotten in touch with her to say he couldn't give
her up and that he loved only her. Since that hadn't
happened, she'd hoped her heart would have started
to let him go, but she'd been wrong. She was wrong
about a lot of things.

Finally the big wall clock indicated that it was quitting time. She'd planned to stop at the grocery store
on her way home, but she changed her mind. There
must be something in her refrigerator she could fix
for supper.

When she drove into the complex, she noticed a
black luxury sedan sitting in the visitor parking lot.
The car made her think of Stuart and wonder whether
he missed her or was annoyed by the impetuous way
she had left. A week ago she had sent a polite note
with her address and phone number, thanking him and
Deidre for their hospitality, but she hadn't gotten a
reply.

She unlocked the door of her apartment and went
inside. Through the partially open blinds covering the
patio slider, she could see a figure sitting at the out-
door table!

Sarah froze.

At least the sliding door was still locked. Whoever
was sitting out there had apparently walked around
the outside of the building.

She recalled the black car. Was it possible that Stuart had come to visit her? Cautiously Sarah went over
to the patio door and peeked through the blinds.

Ryan! Her first thought was that something must

have happened to her grandfather or to Jessica. As she fumbled with the lock, he looked up, sunglasses hiding his eyes.

"Is Stuart all right?" she asked as soon as she got the door open.

"Yes," he exclaimed, getting to his feet and tucking the sunglasses into his shirt pocket. "Stuart's fine."

Sarah drew in a deep breath. Ryan looked wonderful in dark slacks and a light-blue dress shirt with the sleeves rolled up. Her heart was thundering in her chest like a herd of wild horses. Distractedly she wished she'd taken the time to run a comb through her hair and freshen her lip gloss before she'd left the bank.

He jammed his hands into the pockets of his slacks and studied her through narrowed eyes. She was painfully aware of the short flowered cotton skirt she wore with an inexpensive knit top and sandals. Why hadn't she worn one of her tailored dresses to work today? They looked so much more professional, even if it did cost the earth to have them dry cleaned.

"How have you been?" he asked.

She could have stood there and stared at him for an hour, but the sun was out and it radiated uncomfortably off the cement patio. He looked cool and relaxed, but the heat was getting to Sarah.

"Would you like to come in?" she asked. "I have some lemonade."

He shrugged. "Thanks. Sounds good."

"How long have you been waiting?" she asked as he followed her inside.

Quickly she grabbed some mail she'd left scattered across the kitchen table and stacked it neatly. At least the dishes were done and her bed was made. The thought of him seeing her bedroom sent fresh heat that had nothing to do with the sun flowing through her.

"I've been here about a half hour," he replied as she managed to pour the lemonade in her best glasses without spilling it and handed him one.

He glanced around the open floor plan of the compact kitchen-dining-living room. "This is nice."

Sarah figured he was only being polite, but she had gone to some effort to fix the place up and she was proud of it. "Thank you." She led the way to the couch and sat down on one end.

"Have you heard from Jessica?" she asked after he'd joined her. Perhaps that was why he had come.

He took a long swallow of his lemonade while she watched the muscles of his throat work, and then he set the glass on the end table. "No. She's still incognito."

"That must be difficult for you," Sarah said.

He arched one brow in silent query. "Why is that?"

Did she have to spell it out? "Is that why you're here, because she hasn't showed up and Stuart is getting impatient for you to marry one of us?" she blurted, no longer caring if Ryan knew she'd been eavesdropping.

He looked genuinely astonished. "What are you talking about?"

"I tried to explain my feelings in the note I left you, but I didn't have much time. I heard you and Stuart talking," she admitted. "I know I shouldn't have listened, but I did."

Ryan was frowning. "Wait a minute. I sure as hell don't remember you *explaining* anything in your note except that you didn't need me anymore to get what you wanted." He leaned forward, his gray eyes bleak. "Tell me, did you think wishing me luck with Jessica was a nice touch?"

It was Sarah's turn to be confused. "I didn't say that!"

"Maybe you just don't remember."

Sarah shook her head in denial. "Why would I write that when I was hoping you'd decide it mattered to you who you married, even if it made no difference to Stuart?"

Ryan's frown deepened. He dug a piece of paper from his pocket. "Here's the note," he said. "Read it for yourself."

Sarah glanced at the unfamiliar handwriting, fury setting in when she read the cruel words. "This isn't the note I left for you. I've never seen it before."

He blew out a breath. "Deidre gave it to me when I came looking for you after I got done talking with Stuart."

"I gave her a note for you, but this isn't it."

"Then I don't understand why you left," he said, stuffing the paper back into his pocket. "Since you were eavesdropping, you must have heard me tell Stuart that I have no intentions of marrying Jessica.''

His words stunned Sarah. A tiny flicker of hope pushed aside her anger at Deidre for switching notes. She must still have been scheming for Ryan to get together with her daughter.

"No, I didn't hear you say that," Sarah admitted, remembering how she had fled even though they were still talking.

He shifted closer and took her hand. "You should have stuck around. I made it pretty clear which twin I'm in love with."

"Which one?" Sarah had forgotten to breathe. She was too busy soaking in the warm approval in his eyes and the way his mouth had relaxed into the beginnings of a smile.

He tucked his finger under her chin and lifted it gently. "A very wise woman once told me that love is the only good reason for marriage. You know, I think she was right. I fell for you before I knew who you were. I fought it, because love wasn't part of my plan, but I couldn't help myself. Then I found out you weren't who I thought." A gleam of laughter appeared in his gaze. "Hell, it turned out you weren't who *you* thought, either. It took me a little while to deal with that, longer than it should have, I admit, but it's kind of a shock when you kidnap someone and then find out she's not who you expected, but then it turns out she sort of is after all." He shook his head woefully. "See why I was confused?"

If Sarah hadn't been so anxious to hear what else

he had to say, she might have laughed. "I hadn't really looked at the situation from that angle."

Ryan stuck his free hand into the pocket of his slacks. The last glimmer of humor vanished from his expression and his grip on her hand tightened. "I asked you this once before," he said as her heart began to slam against her ribs. "I called you by the wrong name, so I want to get it right this time. Sarah Daniels, will you marry me?"

Sarah's throat tightened as she tried not to cry. She would always remember the way he had proposed to her back in the woods, but this time was even better.

"Yes," she whispered, her heart brimming over with happiness. "I'll marry you no matter what name you choose to call me."

He opened the hand he'd withdrawn from his pocket. Resting on his palm was a ring. Smiling into her eyes, he slipped it onto her finger.

"If you don't like it, I'll get you something else," he said, "but when I saw this, it reminded me of you."

"It's beautiful." Sarah gazed down at the lovely emerald framed with diamonds. "It's perfect. I'm so lucky."

Ryan took her into his arms. "No, you're perfect," he said softly, the love shining in his eyes. "And I'm the lucky one, my Sarah."

Then he kissed her.

* * * * *

Here's a sneak peek at

THE BRIDAL QUEST,

by Jennifer Mikels,
in the next installment of
the exciting new miniseries,

HERE COME THE BRIDES,

available in November 2000,
only from Silhouette Special Edition!

and demanded

Chapter One

"Lady, what are you doing there?"

Jessica Walker spun around and away from the handwritten Help Wanted sign she'd been reading. Standing in the shadowed light of the moon, she shrank against the window of the local diner behind her. Her heart pounding, she fought panic, and peered at the man approaching her from his car. If only she could see his face.

Darkness shadowed the stairs, but while he climbed them, she gathered an impression. He was tall and broad-shouldered, not old, maybe in his thirties. She saw no more. A beam of light flashed in her eyes, blinding her. She squinted, then looked away from the flashlight he held. "Who are you?" she demanded back to veil fear. It skittered up her spine as he took another step closer.

"The sheriff. Sam Dawson."

Almost on top of her, he lowered the flashlight. She stared hard, saw it now, the badge pinned to a pale, maybe khaki-colored shirt. He was the last person she wanted to see.

"Why don't you tell me what you're doing out here?"

She drew a shaky, but calmer breath. She got an image of a good-looking man. Great-looking, she realized when he stepped into the faint light from the diner's sign. He had a face of angles from the sharp cheekbones and the bridge of the long, straight nose to the strongly defined jaw. Briefly her eyes stopped on his lips, on the full bottom one. "I saw the Help Wanted sign on the window when the bus drove by the diner," she finally answered.

"You came by bus?"

"Yes." She'd thought Thunder Lake, Nevada might be a good place to hide when she'd left her Ferrari in a parking lot just blocks from the bus station. Earlier, while riding by, a neon sign for Herb's Diner had caught her eye. By the time she'd gotten off the bus, the diner had closed, and darkness shielded a view of the inside.

"Step over here," he said, urging her out of the shadows and toward the diner's door and the light.

Her heart beat harder as she followed his suggestion and plastered her back to the door.

"Where did you come from?"

Panic rushed her again. What if he asked for identification? "West of here."

"West? That's pretty vague." A thread of annoyance entered his voice. "West of Thunder Lake? West of Hoover Dam?" He inclined his head as if trying to see her eyes. "West of what, mystery lady?"

"I'm not." Her fingers tightened on her purse strap.

"Not what?"

"A mystery lady." Nerves. She could hear them in the stiffness of her voice.

"What's your name?"

"Scott. Jessica Scott." *Oh, please don't ask for identification.* How dumb not to have thought of this problem before she'd taken off. She'd left, deciding to use a maid's last name, bordered on idiotic if she didn't want anyone to find her. But her only identification carried the name Walker. She hurried words to steer conversation her way. "I wanted to read the sign, see if there was a time on the door. I planned to get here early, be the first one applying for the job."

He sort of laughed. The husky soft sound whispered over her, relaxed her quicker than anything else might have. "There won't be a crowd rushing the door for the waitress job. Don't worry about it."

She needed to act normal. Not make him suspicious. "Oh, that's good."

"You've been a waitress before?"

She nodded. Liar, liar, pants on fire. She could have told him that she possessed a wealth of other skills.

She'd charmed dignitaries during a state dinner at the Governor's house. She'd persuaded a CEO of a major corporation to write a check for her favorite charity. She'd hobnobbed with high society. But she'd never worked a day in her life.

"Are you visiting someone here?"

Questions. How many questions would he ask? "No." She'd chosen the town on a whim. She'd closed her eyes and had drawn a small imaginary circle on the Nevada map. Her well-manicured fingernail had zeroed in on Thunder Lake. She'd thought it sounded peaceful, envisioned huge pines and a deep blue-colored lake. In retrospect, she believed she should have run to a big city in another state instead of a small northern town in Nevada.

For a long moment, his eyes fixed on her face as if memorizing it. Then he took a more relaxed stance. She assumed he'd decided she wasn't planning to break in. "Where are you staying?"

She had no idea. Uneasiness rushing through her again, she dodged his stare. Several hundred feet away, across the street, a sign for a motel flashed like a welcoming beacon in the night. She spotted the vacancy sign. More important were the words below it. Cheapest rates in town. "Over there," she said, pointing. A breeze whipped around her, tossing her hair. No longer paralyzed by fear, as the chilly April air sliced through her, she shivered.

"It's cold. You should go to your room. Though this is a small town, it's still not a good idea to be wandering around so late by yourself."

"Late? Nine o'clock is late?" Obviously the streets rolled up early.

She supposed she looked as amazed by his words as she sounded because he offered an explanation. "It is in Thunder Lake. Except in summer when tourists come, it's a quiet town. People work hard here, get up early, go to bed early."

She heard pride in his voice when he talked. Without knowing a thing about Sheriff Sam Dawson, she'd make a guess that he was born and raised here.

"Sounds as if you're used to big-city living."

Instinctively she tensed. Be careful, she warned herself. He was trained to read between lines. "I'll— I should go," she said with a wave of her hand in the direction of her motel. Leaving quickly seemed the smartest thing to do. She gave him a semblance of a smile, hoping it would convince him that she wasn't a fugitive on the run.

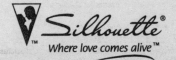

You're not going to believe this offer!

In October and November 2000, buy any two Harlequin or Silhouette books and save $10.00 off future purchases, or buy any three and save $20.00 off future purchases!

Just fill out this form and attach 2 proofs of purchase (cash register receipts) from October and November 2000 books and Harlequin will send you a coupon booklet worth a total savings of $10.00 off future purchases of Harlequin and Silhouette books in 2001. Send us 3 proofs of purchase and we will send you a coupon booklet worth a total savings of $20.00 off future purchases.

Saving money has never been this easy.

I accept your offer! Please send me a coupon booklet:

Name: _____

Address: _____ City: _____

State/Prov.: _____ Zip/Postal Code: _____

Optional Survey!

In a typical month, how many Harlequin or Silhouette books would you buy <u>new</u> at retail stores?

☐ Less than 1   ☐ 1   ☐ 2   ☐ 3 to 4   ☐ 5+

Which of the following statements best describes how you <u>buy</u> Harlequin or Silhouette books? Choose one answer only that <u>best</u> describes you.

☐ I am a regular buyer and reader

☐ I am a regular reader but buy only occasionally

☐ I only buy and read for specific times of the year, e.g. vacations

☐ I subscribe through Reader Service but also buy at retail stores

☐ I mainly borrow and buy only occasionally

☐ I am an occasional buyer and reader

Which of the following statements best describes how you <u>choose</u> the Harlequin and Silhouette series books you buy <u>new</u> at retail stores? By "series," we mean books within a particular line, such as *Harlequin PRESENTS* or *Silhouette SPECIAL EDITION*. Choose one answer only that <u>best</u> describes you.

☐ I only buy books from my favorite series

☐ I generally buy books from my favorite series but also buy books from other series on occasion

☐ I buy some books from my favorite series but also buy from many other series regularly

☐ I buy all types of books depending on my mood and what I find interesting and have no favorite series

---

Please send this form, along with your cash register receipts as proofs of purchase, to:
In the U.S.: Harlequin Books, P.O. Box 9057, Buffalo, NY 14269
In Canada: Harlequin Books, P.O. Box 622, Fort Erie, Ontario L2A 5X3
(Allow 4-6 weeks for delivery) Offer expires December 31, 2000.   PHQ4002

Silhouette® —

where love comes alive—online...

eHARLEQUIN.com

your romantic life

—Romance 101
♥ Guides to romance, dating and flirting.

—Dr. Romance
♥ Get romance advice and tips from our expert, Dr. Romance.

—Recipes for Romance
♥ How to plan romantic meals for you and your sweetie.

—Daily Love Dose
♥ Tips on how to keep the romance alive every day.

—Tales from the Heart
♥ Discuss romantic dilemmas with other members in our Tales from the Heart message board.

SINTL1

COMING NEXT MONTH

#1357 A MAN ALONE—Lindsay McKenna
Morgan's Mercenaries: Maverick Hearts
Captain Thane Hamilton was a loner who'd closed off his heart long ago.
But when this strapping Marine returned home to recover from his most
dangerous mission, he couldn't deny the fierce desire unassuming nurse
Paige Black was arousing with her tender loving care....

#1358 THE RANCHER NEXT DOOR—Susan Mallery
Lone Star Canyon
A long-standing feud had forced rancher Jack Darby to end his
clandestine affair with sweetly innocent Katie Fitzgerald. Now he
wanted to win her back. But he'd have to do more than unleash his pent-
up passion—he'd have to prove that this time he'd be hers forever!

#1359 SOPHIE'S SCANDAL—Penny Richards
Rumor Has It...
One unforgettable night long ago, Sophie Delaney had given rakish
Reed Hardisty the precious gift of her virginity. But then their scheming
families cruelly wrenched them apart. Now, years later, was it possible
for these high school sweethearts to recapture the love they once shared?

#1360 THE BRIDAL QUEST—Jennifer Mikels
Here Come the Brides
Runaway heiress Jessica Walker went into hiding as a nanny for
handsome Sam Dawson's darling daughters. But could the sheriff's little
matchmakers convince Jessica their daddy was the husband she'd always
longed for?

#1361 BABY OF CONVENIENCE—Diana Whitney
Stork Express
In a matter of days, Laura Michaels had gone from struggling single
mom to married woman living in a mansion! But could Laura and her
adorable son transform Royce Burton—her stubbornly sexy husband of
convenience—into a devoted husband and father?

#1362 JUST EIGHT MONTHS OLD...—Tori Carrington
Rugged bounty hunter Chad Hogan had lost the fiery beauty he'd fallen
for when he'd given her a sports car instead of an engagement ring. And
when Hannah McGee reappeared with a beautiful baby—*his* baby girl—
he was determined to claim his woman and child.

CMN1000